no WORD for
GOODBYE

Books by Mignon F. Ballard

Augusta Goodnight Mysteries
Angel at Troublesome Creek
An Angel to Die For
Shadow of an Angel
The Angel Whispered Danger
Too Late for Angels
The Angel and the Jabberwocky Murders
Hark! the Herald Angel Screamed

Miss Dimple Kilpatrick Mysteries
Miss Dimple Disappeares
Miss Dimple Rallies To The Cause
Miss Dimple Suspects: A Mystery
Miss Dimple Picks A Peck Of Trouble
Miss Dimple and the Slightly Bewildered Angel

Stand Alone Mysteries
Aunt Matilda's Ghost
Raven Rock
Cry at Dusk
How Still We See Thee Lie
(previously published as *Deadly Promise*)
The Widow's Woods
Final Curtain
Minerva Cries Murder
The War in Sallie's Station
The Christmas Cottage
No Word for Goodbye

no WORD for
GOODBYE

MIGNON F. BALLARD

BellaRosaBooks

BellaRosaBooks

NO WORD FOR GOODBYE
ISBN 978-1-62268-165-5
First Edition

Also available in e-book form: ISBN 978-1-62268-166-2.

Cover illustration by Marilyn Lindholm and Mignon F. Ballard

BellaRosaBooks and logo are trademarks of Bella Rosa Books.

10   9   8   7   6   5   4   3   2   1

In honor of the Cherokee, who were here first.

Acknowledgements:

For my friends, David Gomez, Ranger at New Echota Historical Site, for his patience and cooperation in the research for this book; and computer wizard Jess Shirley for guiding me through the technical jungle, thank you!

Chapter One

I didn't want to go there. And then, I didn't want to leave. Neither did any of the others.

But they had no choice.

Looking back on that time I remember the creaking and bumping of wagon wheels on the furrowed road to New Echota, the choking swarms of dust that invaded our hair, our clothing. Even the food tasted of grit. But most of all, I remember the great hurtful lump wedged just below my heart.

My name is Nell Kiziah Webb, and this is how it began.

It was all the fault of the Willinghams' cat. If that cat hadn't teased our dog Gulliver, then Gulliver wouldn't have chased him, causing Papa's horse, Liberty, to rear. Papa wouldn't have ended up with a broken leg, and I wouldn't have ended up a million miles away—or at least that how it seemed.

What if it was only a dream? Maybe if I thought long enough, hard enough I would be in my own yard, pebbles crunching under my feet as I ran the familiar path that circled the garden, Lucy calling to me in her warm apple pudding voice to hurry and wash my hands for dinner.

Closing my eyes, I thought of the rose, the pink climbing rose that hugged the trellis over the back door. My mother had planted it before I was born and its velvety scent sweetened the air from May through autumn. Before I left, I had buried my face in its petals and breathed so deeply and so long it almost made me dizzy. The rose was a part of me, a part of home. I couldn't take it with me, but I could remember. I had to remember.

The wagon rocked and jolted over a rut in the road and I covered my nose against the dust. Behind us Aunt Sadie's milk cow Mabel let out a bellow to let us know she was ready for her supper and a place to rest for the night. So was I.

"I know, old girl, but it shouldn't be long now," Uncle Amos called back to her. "We should pick up the Hightower Trail at Etowah before dark." He pulled the two mules, Jenny and Old Sue, to the side of the road so I could climb down and untie the cow to let her graze. We had left home almost two weeks before but she still smelled of the warm stable and sweet-scented hay she left behind. I patted her ruffled brown neck while she foraged the dusty weeds beside the road. We had replenished our water supply along the way whenever we came to a stream or a spring. Miles back at Hickory Log we filled our barrel from the well and drank our fill of its icy sweetness, but I didn't know how much was left of that.

Although I was in no hurry to get to our destination, I hoped we would soon reach the Etowah River where Mabel and the two mules could drink. If we were lucky, Uncle Amos might catch a few fish for Aunt Sadie to coat in corn meal and fry for our supper.

Dusk came earlier now in late October and soon darkness would creep in from either side. I drew my cloak about me, dreading another night in this strange wooded place where frogs, owls and other forest creatures called to each other. At least I hoped they were forest creatures. We had left the protection of the Federal Government when we entered the Cherokee Nation at Vann's Ferry days before, and although the forest pressed around us for much of our journey, in daylight I could see my surroundings. In the dark each curious sound became a threat.

Papa had said the Cherokees were a civilized tribe and I had no need to worry. The tiny village of New Echota was modeled like some of our own, he told me, where the people gardened, raised their own livestock, and lived in the type of home I might find familiar.

But I had read Mr. Cooper's *The Last of the Mohicans* and knew the stories of settlers being scalped, kidnapped, and massacred. How could we be sure the Cherokees weren't like that too?

And I was going to live among them.

Back in the wagon I watched red dust rise in clouds as we bounced over the furrowed road. In our wake, tall yellowing grass nodded and bowed, closing in the trail behind us, shutting me away from the village of Athens and the only home I've ever known. From my seat on Aunt Sadie's trunk, I tied my day cap under my chin in an attempt to shut out the dust. The trunk was filled with quilts tucked around Aunt Sadie's special dishes— the ones with the swirly blue roses that had belonged to her mother.

Aunt Sadie and her husband Amos aren't really my aunt and uncle, but I've always addressed them that way. The Colliers have been our friends and neighbors for as long as I can remember and are as close as any relatives I know. Now, they were on their way to live near their daughter and her family in Tennessee, and I'm traveling with them until we reach New Echota in the northern end of our state.

If only Miss Mary Rose hadn't married and gone to live in Augusta, or if Lucy hadn't gotten so old and "down in the back," as she calls it, I could still be back in Athens in our house on Hancock Street. Miss Mary Rose was my governess who had been with us since I was a small child, and I liked her just fine, even though she did take a notion to marry Mr. Everett and leave me to live in Augusta. She wore her shiny brown hair in two braided loops that sometimes came loose and curled in little twists around her ears, and she liked reading fairy stories—especially "Snow White"—almost as much as I did.

"Just think," Miss Mary Rose reminded me, "not only do the Cherokees have their own alphabet, but their own newspaper as well, and you'll be attending school right there in the capital of the Cherokee Nation."

But Miss Mary Rose wasn't the one who was going to live in Indian Territory where I was sure to be scalped and chopped into little pieces with a tomahawk. Well, it would serve them all right if I died.

Although I'd rather not.

After having me christened Nell Kizia, which is about the ugliest name I can think of, my mother up and died of pneumonia when I was only a few months old. Lucy was the one who rocked me and sang to me, holding me close on her soft lap, the one who taught me my prayers and stayed up nights nursing me when I was sick.

Papa tried to explain that Lucy was getting up in years, and wasn't able to get around like she used to, but she would still be there in her little house behind ours when I came home again. But would she? Was I ever going to see her again?

And my poor papa! It took two men to carry him inside after he was thrown from his horse. A neighbor happened to be passing by, and he and Lucy's son Andrew laid him on the big mahogany table in the dining room. Thank goodness Dr. Means lived just around the corner and I pulled up my skirts and ran for him as fast as my legs could carry me. Lucy made me go outside while the doctor set Papa's leg; she didn't say so, but I knew it was because she didn't want me to hear him holler. I went out and sat under the sweetshrub bush behind the barn and held Gulliver on my lap so he couldn't hear anything either.

Later, after Dr. Means set Papa's leg and tied it to wooden splits with wide strips of cloth, the men moved the chaise lounge into his study from the parlor and made him a bed in there. The doctor said Papa was lucky as it was a clean break below the knee but it was going to take some time to heal.

I wasn't aware of it at the time, but the thing that seemed to concern Papa most was what to do with me. I don't know why because I wasn't the one with the broken leg.

A week or so after his fall, Papa called me into his study to tell me he had arranged with my mother's

brother, John Wheeler, and his wife Nancy, to have me
live with them and attend school until he could find
another governess.

Uncle John was a printer who had been brought to
New Echota from Brainerd in Tennessee to assist with
the printing of the Cherokee newspaper, *The Phoenix*.
While there, he met and married a Cherokee, Nancy
Watie, sister to the editor, Elias Boudinot. He and his
wife and baby lived in a cottage not far from the print
shop, Papa went on to say.

Papa's study smelled of candle wax and old books
and I had always liked the scent of it, but that day I
clamped a hand over my nose and tried not to breathe.
Well water ran through my bones and it seemed that
somebody else stood there in my place.

Papa was propped up on pillows with his injured leg
elevated on a folded quilt. "Sit down, Bella Nella," he
invited me, nodding to a chair beside his bed. And so I
did. He hadn't called me by that silly name since I was
five—unless I was really sick.

I was sick now.

I had never met my uncle John, but a portrait of
him and my mother as children hung in an oval frame in
our parlor. My uncle, who looked to be about four, had
tousled blond curls and wore a blousy blue suit with a
big white collar. Mother, three years older, stood beside
him in a ruffled white dress with a wide pink sash. She
had light brown hair like mine and held a kitten in her
arms. I had always wondered what the kitten's name
was. Maybe my uncle could tell me.

But that wasn't what I wanted to hear just then.
"*Why?*" I said. "Why do I have to leave? Why can't I
stay here with you and Lucy and Thomas?"

My brother Tom just turned sixteen and is studying arts and sciences at Franklin College a few blocks away. He could shinny up a tree as fast as a squirrel, mount a horse in midstride, and whittle a whistle out of a willow stick, but now that he's all grown-up he doesn't have time for those things. Or me.

Papa frowned. "Lucy's not as young as she used to be, Nell. She's not able to do all the things she did in the past, and we shouldn't expect her to. And, as you know, your brother is busy with his studies at the college." He sighed and shifted his position a bit against the pillows. "You'll soon become a young lady, and you're going to need a woman's influence until I can make other arrangements."

"But, Papa, I don't even know Uncle John. Why can't I stay with Aunt Ida?" Aunt Ida is Papa's aunt who lives just down the road from us and sleeps in her chair most of the time. She claims she's sewing, but I never understood how a person could sew with her eyes shut.

Sighing, Papa shook his head. "I promised your dear mother I would see that you had a proper education, and I mean to do just that. It won't do for you to fall behind in your studies, and I understand from your uncle that a Miss Sawyer has come from Brainerd to teach in the school there."

I gripped the arms of the chair until I could feel its imprint on my palms. "You want me to go to school with *Indians?*"

Papa turned to face me, and reached out to enclose my hand in his. Although I could tell his leg was hurting him, he smiled and assured me I had nothing to worry about. "Your uncle seems to have high regard for this teacher, and you'll be living with him and your aunt

Nancy within walking distance of the school."

Choking back tears, I turned away. How could he do this to me? "She's *not* my aunt! She's—"

Papa's voice was firm but gentle. "Your uncle's wife is from an honorable Cherokee family, Nell, and her brother, Elias, is married to a fine young woman he met while in school in Connecticut. I understand they live nearby."

Papa looked at me with eyes so sad I thought he was going to cry. "I heard back from your uncle by messenger yesterday to let me know that he and your aunt are expecting you and will be looking forward to your arrival."

I studied the design in the carpet at my feet where vine-like leaves twisted around some kind of flower. I had nothing to say.

"It's only for a little while, and as soon as I can find someone to replace Miss Mary Rose, you'll be home before you know it. Please try to understand," he said. "It's not that I *want* you to leave."

Then why?

I turned and ran from the room, past Papa's mahogany writing desk, tall shelves filled with musty books, the plaster bust of Homer with a chip off his nose, and over the familiar carpet with swirly flowers the color of blackberry wine, through the hall, out the door, and across the lawn.

Lucy sat in her bentwood rocking chair sewing squares of cloth into what would become a quilt, and I threw myself on her lap and cried. She didn't say a word. She didn't have to.

Chapter Two

I woke to the smell of coffee . . . and something else . . . something good, and crawled from my pallet between Aunt Sadie's trunk and her butter churn to find her stewing apples over a fire. We had bought them from a Cherokee farmer a few days before and they were a welcome addition to our diet of corncakes, hominy, and, now and then, bacon.

It was still dark as Uncle Amos wanted to get an early start, hoping to reach Oothcaloga before the rain set in. Rain wasn't far away, he promised. He could feel it in his bones. The night before we had camped beside the Etowah after joining the Hightower Trail. Now a cold mist hovered over the ground. Shivering, I stood close to the fire watching Aunt Sadie turn corncakes in her cast iron spider.

The sooty black pan sat on three legs over hot coals while the cakes turned golden-brown with crisp lacy edges. I juggled mine from hand to hand until it was cool enough to eat along with a helping of apples and a warm frothy mug of Mabel's milk.

"How much farther?" I asked Uncle Amos, after finally having worked up the courage to ask.

I fanned away the smoke when he doused what was left of our fire. "With luck, we should get there by tomorrow," he said.

Tomorrow. We were almost there. Reluctantly, I climbed onto the wagon seat beside Aunt Sadie. The world as I knew it was about to end.

Smiling, she drew me to her in a brief hug. "Your uncle John is going to be so happy to see you, Nell. I know how much your sweet mother loved him, and I know he's going to love you, too."

The mules started off with a jerk and I held to Aunt Sadie with one hand and the seat with the other. My breakfast sat like a big chunk of rock in my stomach.

"Aunt Ida said Papa should be ashamed to send me away like this," I told her. "She said all Indians are savages—even the women, and I'll be lucky to come back alive."

Aunt Sadie laughed. "Your aunt Ida thinks any woman's a savage if she doesn't wear three petticoats and a corset over her shift. I should hope you'd have better sense than to listen to her." She gave my arm a squeeze. "We're about to have an adventure, Nell, a *big* adventure—all of us, and much of it depends on what we make of it."

I didn't remember anyone asking me if I was ready for an adventure, but if they had, I would've said, no, thank you, not just yet. But of course I wasn't asked.

If only Papa had just given in and married the Widow McGinnis, I would probably still be back in Athens. She lived right down the road from us and anyone could see she was sweet on Papa. She was always bringing us flowers from her garden and some of her "special" cakes. The cakes were as hard as marble and tasted like chalk, and it was impossible not to stare at the long hairs on her chin, but if she'd married Papa it would've made things a lot easier for me.

I guess I must have sighed because Aunt Sadie gave me a look that clearly said she didn't like what she was hearing.

"Sometimes people have to do things they would rather not do," she told me. "You must know your Papa would prefer to have you stay at home, but he won't be able to be up and about for a while, and with Miss Mary Rose gone, you'll need help keeping up with your studies."

She gave me one of those smiles grown people give when you know they really don't believe what they're saying. "Now, don't you worry. I'm sure he'll find a new governess soon."

Papa was one of the best lawyers in Athens—well, *the* best as far as I was concerned, so he was able to continue in his practice from his study. He also taught languages at the College, but that would have to wait. I don't know why he wouldn't be able to teach me until he could find another governess, but when I asked him that, he just laughed and said he doubted if he could keep up with me.

It turned out Uncle Amos was right about the rain—or at least his bones were. Just before noon thunder clattered in the distance and lightning zigzagged across the sky. Jenny and old Sue whinnied in protest, and I wasn't happy about it either as rain blew against the canvas while the wagon slogged through trenches of red clay.

After a while, Uncle Amos pulled off the road into a patch of woods to give the animals a rest, but I was glad when he said it was time to get on the trail again after the rain slacked a short time later. Even though the canopy of trees gave us some protection from the wind and rain, I felt more vulnerable there.

I guess it had to happen sooner or later. We had hoped to reach Oothcaloga before dark, but were on the road again for probably less than an hour when one of the back wheels hit a deep muddy gash in the road sending all of us lurching forward.

To lighten the load, I got out and stood beside the wagon and Aunt Sadie took the reins while Uncle Amos urged the mules forward. Still, the wagon refused to budge.

"It's no use," Uncle Amos announced after examining the mired wheel. "I'll have to try something else. This is only making it worse."

I didn't think it could get any worse, but that was before the Indian appeared.

He came upon us on his horse from the opposite direction and watched us silently from the side of the road. Not knowing his intentions, Aunt Sadie reached out and pulled me close and I clung to her hand while my heart beat a drum roll in my chest. Then, quickly dismounting, the man tied his horse to a sapling and went about helping Uncle Amos cover the water-filled rut with pine boughs. He was slender in build, looked to be a few inches taller than Uncle Amos, and was dressed in a buckskin hunting shirt fringed at the bottom and trousers of brown homespun.

Although the man didn't speak, Uncle Amos seemed to know what he had in mind because he directed Aunt Sadie and me to pull the team from the front while the two men pushed the wagon from behind. It took a few tries until the wagon finally bumped free, but before we had time to thank him, the stranger mounted his horse and was gone.

My legs were so weak Uncle Amos had to give me a boost into the wagon, and to my surprise, I suddenly began to cry.

"My goodness, child, why are you crying?" Aunt Sadie said. "That fellow only stopped to help. He never meant to hurt us."

But we didn't know that, I thought. Instead, I blotted my tears with the back of my hand and said I guess I was just crying from relief.

We had seen Cherokee travelers as well as whites along the trail since we entered the Nation, but the incident with the wagon wheel caught us alone, and helpless—or at least it had seemed that way to me.

We found the road, usually well maintained by the Cherokees, difficult in places after the recent hard rain, but we managed to make it to Oothcaloga before nightfall in time to have supper at the tavern there.

"Oh, Nell, look at us!" Aunt Sadie sighed, pointing to the hems of our mud-spattered skirts, and while Uncle Amos led the animals to the stable for the night, she managed to sponge off the worst of it so we could dry before the fire.

At a long table with other travelers, we feasted on venison and roasted hog with sweet potatoes, squash, applesauce, and something called Indian bread that had been baked in the ashes. I welcomed the chance to eat at a table again but would just as soon Aunt Sadie hadn't reminded me that the next time I sat down to eat would be at Aunt Nancy's table in New Echota.

It was hard to leave the warmth of the room with its comforting smell of food and cheerful fire, but there were no accommodations for the three of us to stay the night so we retired to the wagon. A chill wind had blown the rain away but the weather had turned colder and Aunt Sadie took extra quilts from her trunk to help keep out the cold.

With a full stomach, and wrapped in a downy quilt, I burrowed into my pallet and closed my eyes. When I woke in the morning we would leave on the last leg of our journey to New Echota. Would I ever get to sleep?

I had almost drifted off when I heard Uncle Amos speak. "It's a good thing John Wheeler finally agreed to that oath of allegiance or he'd be spending the next few years in Milledgeville."

I knew Milledgeville was our state capital, but what could Uncle John be doing there? And why did he have to take an oath?

Aunt Sadie's voice was hardly more than a whisper. "It's wrong what the state's trying to do. I hope it won't all come about."

"If the government gets its way, the Cherokees will be relocated," Uncle Amos said. "Andrew Jackson will see to it."

What did they mean by that? And what did President Jackson have to do with it?

Yawning, I buried my head in the quilt. I would ask them first thing in the morning.

Chapter Three

We woke to a dreary world. The tavern offered a break-fast of oatmeal, eggs, and bacon but I couldn't eat a bite. Afterward, waiting for Uncle Amos to hitch up the wagon, Aunt Sadie and I stood on the porch and looked out on a landscape of gray. Dark clouds of trees hovered over the trail; shadowy underbrush cloaked the roadsides, and it was impossible to see more than a few feet through a curtain of fog. It seemed the whole earth was in mourning.

Uncle Amos wasted no time in getting away as they still had several days journey ahead to reach Knoxville. I hoped the two of them would at least spend one night at New Echota but he explained that they wanted to put as many miles as they could behind them after leaving me with my uncle.

I crawled into the back of the wagon and read a little in my book of *Grimm's Fairy Tales*, but the stories made me even sadder. I knew just how Cinderella and Hansel and Gretel must have felt.

"Shouldn't be long now!" Aunt Sadie called from her seat up front. "We ought to be there soon."

Reluctantly, I peeked out the back to see a sun-streaked road behind us as looming trees gave way to fields of weathered corn stalks and cows grazing behind zigzag fences. Turning foliage of oaks, sumac, black gum and persimmon colored the hillsides, and now and then a log cabin or small white farmhouse became visible from the road.

The way looked wider now as we passed travelers on foot, horseback, and wagons going in both directions. Most looked to be Cherokee, although many dressed as we did.

Earlier at breakfast I had asked Aunt Sadie about their conversation the night before. "Why was Uncle John in Milledgeville? Is President Jackson really going to move the Cherokees?"

She only sighed and shook her head. "We hope it won't come to that, Nell. I don't think you need to be concerned about it just now."

Then when? I wanted to ask but she went on to tell me that as a white man, John Wheeler had to take an oath of allegiance to the state in order to live in the Cherokee Nation.

"Will I have to do that, too?" I wanted to know.

Aunt Sadie laughed, then grew serious. "No, sweet child, that won't be asked of you. It's too soon to tell about all these goings-on with the state, but I expect you'll hear more about it from your aunt Nancy and uncle John."

"Does Papa know?" I burrowed cold hands under my cape as a stiff wind whipped around the corner.

She didn't answer right away and so I asked again.

She frowned. "Yes, he's very much aware of the situation, Nell, and I believe he feels strongly about the Cherokee cause.

"I suppose it's all right to tell you this now, but your father had considered running for the state legislature before that accident with his leg." Sighing, she shook her head. "Of course, that will be impossible now."

Now, Aunt Sadie made her way slowly into the back of the wagon. "We shouldn't be far from New Echota, and it's not too soon to start getting your things together. You don't want to leave anything behind."

My spirits plunged well-deep. I could no longer wish it away. The time I'd been dreading was here. Silently I worked beside Aunt Sadie to gather the things I'd brought along. Aside from a few books, pens, writing paper, and my treasured watercolor paints, I had only a valise with my clothing, carefully packed by Lucy as space was limited.

I had chosen my new green striped dress with the gigot (sometimes called leg of mutton) sleeves; two morning dresses in dark serviceable colors with white cotton capelets, or pelerines, and chemises to wear beneath.

Aunt Sadie paused to inspect the contents. "Do you have enough petticoats? And what about a shift or two for night wear?"

I assured her they were included, along with two linen aprons, my one pair of black kid leather slippers, an extra pair of boots, and both black and white wool stockings. I had brought only one bonnet. Papa had been told that if needed, I could purchase another at the small store there.

Jenny and Old Sue slowed, making the turn to New Echota, then picked up their pace as if they knew water and a chance to rest awaited them.

I was afraid to look. In spite of what I'd been told, what if the people lived in teepees and mud huts? What if it was ugly and barren?

It wasn't.

A green carpet of grass, sprinkled with bright autumn leaves, spread in front of us. Here and there, hardwoods yet to turn splashed the area with shade. Several people dipped water from a large spring in the center of the town square and I saw that streets had been laid out much like our own with framed houses scattered about.

A shrill scream startled me so I grabbed onto Aunt Sadie's skirt as though we had been attacked, and was surprised when she began to laugh. "That's not anything you won't see back in Athens," she said, pointing to two children running from a log house nearby.

A young Cherokee boy chased an older girl with a bucket of what looked like apples. The girl ran, braids flying, as he reached in the bucket and threw one, nearly missing her.

We watched as a tall, slender woman I assumed was their mother, called to them from the doorway. Swinging the bucket, the boy turned and slowly made his way to the house while the girl picked up one of the apples and threw it, laughing as it hit him smack in the middle of his back. I found myself laughing too.

Aunt Sadie made her way to the front of the wagon. "Your papa tells us the Wheeler cottage is located near the print shop, so we should see it soon."

"Is that it?" I asked, pointing to a neat two-story frame building in the center of the square.

"I think that might be the council house," Uncle Amos said, looking about. The wagon slowed as we creaked along passing another white-painted home with several outbuildings. Could this be where I was to live? But to my disappointment, we moved on. We soon came upon a small neat building of squared off logs that

Uncle Amos pointed out as the print shop.

"That must be it up ahead!" Aunt Sadie called out.

The neat shingled cottage was surrounded by a split rail fence and shaded by a tree with golden leaves I later learned was hickory. Smoke trailed from a chimney at one end, and a narrow porch bordered the front door with windows on either side. It reminded me of Aunt Ida's house back in Athens.

What if the Wheelers weren't here? What if my uncle and his wife had changed their minds? I wanted to wait in the wagon but Aunt Sadie took me firmly by the hand and led me to the door. It opened before we had knocked.

She had kind eyes and a smile that made me feel that *maybe* things were going to be all right. "I'm Nancy," she said, "and I thought you'd never get here!" Her skin was the color of the tea Lucy pours from Mother's china pot and she wore her sleek black hair in braids around her head. Reaching out both hands to us, she led us inside. The room smelled of nutmeg.

A basket of wood stood next to the fireplace at one end of the room with chairs on either side. "Your uncle John should be home soon and I know he'll be happy to see you," Aunt Nancy said. "Come and get warm by the fire, I imagine you could use some hot cider."

I asked if that was what smelled of nutmeg but she stooped to stir something in a pot cooling on the hearth explaining the spice was in gourd soup made of winter squash, chicken broth and cream. A wooden trestle table with benches on each side stretched in front of the fire. I sat on one of the benches, and, with a sigh, Aunt Sadie sank onto a chair while Uncle Thomas held out his hands to the fire.

Aunt Nancy drew my attention to a cradle in the

corner. "Would you like to meet your new cousin?" she asked. "Her name is Helen."

Of course I would! I hadn't noticed the tiny baby wrapped in a hooded bunting sleeping inside. Except for her rosy face, she might've been a rag doll like the ones Lucy made for me.

"What a tiny little thing!" Aunt Sadie stooped beside her. "I don't remember ours ever being this small. Do you, Amos?"

Uncle Amos, turning to warm his other side before the fire, only smiled and shook his head.

Aunt Nancy laughed. "When Helen's hungry, her cries are anything but dainty.

"She's almost three months old," she told us. "And just wait until you see her smile."

Sipping spicy apple cider from a pewter mug warmed my hands as well as my stomach and I watched Aunt Sadie stretch out her feet to the fire as she drained hers to the last drop. "Well," she said, with a look at Uncle Amos, "I expect we'd best be on our way."

"You'll need something more in your stomach than apple cider before you get back on the road. I hope you'll stay long enough to share soup and corn cakes," Aunt Nancy said.

To my relief, my traveling companions agreed that would be a fine idea. At least it would delay their departure for a little while. Aunt Nancy swung the soup pot over the fire to warm and after clearing away the empty mugs, spread the table with a clean white cloth and took bowls and spoons from a corner cabinet. The dishes in the cupboard had the same pink flowered pattern as our china back in Athens, and I was told it was part of the same set.

"Your mother was given the teapot and the other half of the china," my aunt explained, "and your uncle John, the rest."

Aunt Sadie smiled. "That should help you feel at home, Nell."

But I wasn't at home. I might as well be a million miles away. I smiled back but it felt like my mouth was going to crack. As soon as the meal was over they would be leaving. Earlier, Uncle Amos had unhitched the mules and led the animals to the trough and I knew he was eager to be back on the road.

I couldn't bear to say good-bye when it was time for them to leave so I gave them both a good long hug and tried my best not to cry. Aunt Sadie didn't bother to wipe away her tears as she took my face in her hands. "I know your dear mother is watching over you, Nell Webb. You're going to be just fine."

If my mother had been watching over me, why was I in this place? I stood in the doorway as they drove away, knowing I would never see them again. If I shut my eyes and held my breath, maybe it would keep my feelings from spewing out. Once they began, they might never stop.

I felt Aunt Nancy's hand on my shoulder. "Would you like to see where you're going to sleep?" she asked in a too-bright voice, and I nodded.

I hadn't noticed the small room at the back, divided from the main area by a blue striped curtain. A single bed with four corner posts stood under the small window framed by yellow flowered calico curtains.

"Your uncle John built this bed when we learned little Helen was on the way," my aunt said, "but it will be some time before she's old enough to use it."

I was given drawer space for my things in the handsome cherry chest that stood at the foot of the bed and began to put them away.

"Our neighbor, Kate, should soon be home from school," my aunt told me. "She usually stops by to play with the baby, and I know she's looking forward to meeting you."

I smiled, eager to meet a new friend. "Oh, good! Is she about my age?"

I tried not to show disappointment when I learned Kate was only seven. There's a lot of difference between seven and eleven.

Aunt Nancy must have guessed what I was thinking because she led me aside. "We're fond of Kate. She's a sweet child and adores Helen, but I think I think you're going to be great friends with her cousin, Callie," she told me. "She's just about your age, and you'll meet her tomorrow when you start to school."

Callie, she explained, was the young Cherokee girl who lived with her family in the house we had passed when we arrived. The laughing girl with the braids.

While Aunt Nancy nursed the baby, I collected our empty dishes and put them in a pan to rinse with a pitcher of water as I had seen Lucy do. Later, after water simmered over the fire, we would wash them with lye soap.

Tomorrow I would begin school in this strange new place. I hoped I was going to like Callie. But would she like me?

Chapter Four

It was barely light the next morning when the loud blast of a horn summoned us, and Kate stopped by for me to begin the short walk to the Council House, a two story log building in the center of town. I was glad to have the company of the younger girl. Small, with long braids that bounced, Kate walked like she was listening to music and seemed to have a smile for everyone. Aunt Nancy promised that Kate would introduce me to our teacher and some of the other students, which made it a lot less scary than going there alone.

"I've told Miss Sawyer she'll have a new student," Aunt Nancy said before we left, "so she'll be expecting you."

Kate drew her face into a scowl. "She won't let you move an inch without permission, and you'd better not dare say a word! We might as well be locked away in that prison in Milledgeville like Mr. Worcester and Dr. Butler—and my papa said they would have kept your uncle John there, too!"

"*Katherine*! That's quite enough of that," my aunt said. Her voice softened as she turned to me. "Sophia Sawyer is strict, Nell, but I think you'll find her fair. Why, Kate, you told me your little friend Susanna won a trinket the other day just for memorizing her bible verses."

With an impish smile, Kate shrugged. "Who wants a little old straw horse anyway?"

My aunt shook her head and smiled. "I suppose Susanna did."

I was told we would be required to memorize several bible verses every day and recite them before our studies began. In addition to that, we were to be instructed in reading, spelling, arithmetic, history, writing, and geography.

But what was this about people being locked in prison? "Why would they want to keep Uncle John—" I began, but Aunt Nancy wasted no time ushering us out the door. "Hurry now. You don't want to be late, especially on Nell's first day."

Our boots made scrunching sounds when we walked, leaving silver footprints on the frost-covered ground. "We had school in the Courthouse before the weather turned colder," Kate explained, "but there's no fireplace there so we moved to the Council House. Our parents take time about supplying wood for the fire." I tugged my cloak about me, relieved to see smoke rising from the chimney at the rear of the building.

"There's my friend Susanna," Kate said, waving to a small dark-haired girl who smiled and waved back. Children came from different directions, some in groups and a few walked alone, but all seemed to be hurrying toward the same place.

"That's where the Boudinots live." Kate pointed to the large white house we had passed on our arrival. "Mr. Boudinot's editor of the newspaper but he's not here right now." Her voice dropped to a whisper. "I heard Papa say he's gone to get money so he can keep the paper in print."

I wanted to ask Kate what she meant when she spoke of the men being locked away in prison, but we were joined by Susanna and her brother Daniel who challenged us in a race to school. They all got there before I did. I wasn't in a hurry.

Kate tugged on my arm when we reached the steps. "Come on! Miss Sawyer doesn't like it if we're late."

But I hung back and stepped aside to let the others swarm past. These people didn't look like me; several of the boys wore moccasins and trousers of buckskin, and some spoke a strange language I didn't understand. *What was I doing here?* I clung to the post at the bottom of the steps and wished I were somewhere else. Anywhere else. The porridge I'd eaten earlier flipped around in my stomach like buttermilk in a churn. Was I going to be sick like the time Lucy put me to bed and dosed me with Epsom salt? I sat on the bottom step and buried my face in my hands. If only Lucy were here— but she wasn't here. Lucy was miles and miles away in Athens.

"Hello, I'm Callie, and Miss Sawyer said we're to sit together."

She stood on the step beside me and held out her hand. "I'm Nell," I said, and smiled when I recognized the laughing girl I'd seen the day before. Maybe this wasn't going to be so bad after all, I thought as we walked in together.

I was surprised to see rows of benches facing a raised platform at the front of the room with steps on either side. Our teacher, Miss Sawyer, who didn't seem nearly as harsh as Kate had led me to believe, smiled and introduced herself as she came forward.

"Class, I'd like you to meet your new classmate,

Nell Webb," she told them. "Nell will be staying with her aunt Nancy and Uncle John for a while, and I hope you will make her feel welcome."

About twenty or more students sat in clusters scattered about the room and they all smiled at me, so of course I smiled back. Everyone seemed to be looking at me as if they expected me to say something, so I mumbled hello and wished she would hurry and tell me where to sit. I had thought I'd be placed with those more my age and was surprised when Callie led me to a bench where three small children looked up expectantly. "Miss Sawyer likes for some of us older ones to help teach the others," she whispered. The boy, who looked to be about five, was called Little Will, she told me, and the two small girls were Alice and Mary.

Looking about, I was surprised to see two small Negro boys seated with the other children and wondered why they were there. I had been told that some of the wealthier Cherokees owned slaves, but why would they bring them to school?

The teacher stood at a small table below the platform at the front of the room and called for those who knew them to recite the bible verses she had assigned. Kate's friend Susanna and my seatmate Callie came forward as did several others.

After assigning the verses we were to memorize for the next day, we were told to stand for the hymn and a girl who looked to be about thirteen or fourteen stepped to the front and sang the first line of "How Firm a Foundation." Her voice was strong and sweet with very little accent. This was repeated by the rest of the class and followed by the second line which was sung in the same way until we had completed three stanzas.

"Thank you, Margaret," Miss Sawyer said as the girl stepped back to her seat. "And tomorrow I'd like to see if we can all sing three verses without having to stop between them."

At last something I knew how to do! The hymn was familiar to me because we sang it often in our small Methodist church back home.

Reading was the next order of the day and under our teacher's supervision, Callie and I helped our small charges read from *Alden's Reader*, a well-worn book with stained and dog-eared pages. I noticed that the two Negro children were given books as well and took part in the lessons with the others. The large room, that had felt cold on our arrival, slowly warmed with the wood fire being constantly replenished by one of our class-mates, and I began to relax in the warmth of its fresh woodsy scent. But I wanted to crawl under the bench and hide when Miss Sawyer called me to the front of the room to hear me read. I had never read aloud to a group before and the thought of it made me feel like my insides were melting, so I was relieved when she said I only had to read to her. I know I must have smiled when she opened the bible and asked me to read Psalm 100 as it's one of Papa's favorites and I practically knew it by heart.

Callie told me later the teacher asked me to read so she would know how to place me in the class. Alice and Mary, the two little girls we were helping, read well, although they stumbled over a few words, but Little Will, who spoke more Cherokee than English, seemed puzzled by it all.

While Callie worked with the others, I read to him

from a book of nursery rhymes, but he didn't show much interest until I came to the one about Miss Muffett. I got so involved in enacting the parts of the scary spider and the poor frightened girl that the little boy laughed out loud and Miss Sawyer rapped on her table with a ruler and told us to be quiet.

I saw that Callie was laughing, too, but she was so quiet about it the teacher didn't even notice. Dropping my voice, I moved on to calmer verses and was in the middle of "Baa, Baa, Black Sheep" when I felt a slight tug on my hair and looked up to find Little Will gently stroking the curl at the end of my braid.

"He likes your hair," Callie whispered, and I was glad somebody did as I don't see anything special about plain old brown hair. Little Will's hair was as black and shiny as a pair of new boots and refused to lie down on his head, and his eyes were dark and bright like the pebbles my brother and I used to find in the bottom of the spring.

Miss Sawyer told me I would be excused from the written spelling test the class would be taking from a list of words from *The Blue Back Speller*, but I chose to take it anyway. When we traded papers to grade them, I was relieved to find I had only missed one word: *grief,* and could almost hear Miss Mary Rose reminding me, *Don't forget, Nell, it's i before e, except after c!*

In the months to come I would learn how that word would leave a dark stain on this beautiful place.

Chapter Five

It seemed a long time since we'd last eaten so I was glad when the teacher said it was time for a break. The day had turned warmer and I sat on the steps in the sun and ate the apple, bread and cheese Aunt Nancy had packed for me in a pail. Callie, her brother Joseph, and several others joined me, and although most were shy at first, a few asked questions about my life back in Athens. It made me sad to talk about it, but I didn't want them to know that, so I tried to describe it the best way I could without thinking of the way the sunlight crisscrossed the floor of my room on a summer morning or the yeasty smell of apple fritters sputtering over the kitchen fire.

"Don't you miss your mother?" a small girl asked. "I know I would."

I explained that my mother died when I was a baby and that Lucy, who helped to raise me, was older now and couldn't get around very well. This was met with round-eyed silence. I later learned from Callie that most Cherokees cared for each other's children in the event of a parent's death.

"I hope your poor papa will be better soon!" Callie looked so sad you might have thought it was her own papa who was laid up with a broken leg.

"He's looking forward to getting back on his feet again," I said, hoping to make her feel less glum. "Our neighbor told me when Papa's able, he might even run for the legislature. Of course then he'd have to spend time in Milledgeville," I added.

Well, I didn't expect her reaction to that!

"Oh, that wicked place!" Callie cried out. "Do you think they plan to hold him long?"

The others seemed equally distressed. "Mr. Worcester and Dr. Butler are still locked away," Callie said, "but your uncle took the oath, so they let him come home."

"Uncle John was locked away?" I asked. "Where?"

"In Milledgeville. That's where the penitentiary is." From the look Joseph gave me I could tell he didn't think I had any sense at all.

"But why were they put in prison?"

He shook his head and turned away. "Race you to the well and back!" he called to another boy.

"Why won't you answer me?" I shouted as he ran away, but Joseph didn't look back.

Callie stood below me. "Don't let my brother worry you. Just talking about it makes him angry." She held out a hand. "Let's go sit under the big oak until Miss Sawyer calls us in.

"They held a trial in Lawrenceville," she began when we were seated. "Miss Sawyer told us about it but I've heard my father and mother talking about it too. All three men were found guilty and taken to the pen in Milledgeville."

Poor Uncle John! He never said a word about it at supper last night, but laughed and hugged me, saying how happy he was to have me here.

"Guilty of what?" I leaned against the rough bark of the tree and looked about me. Wisps of smoke trailed from every chimney, and red and gold leaves littered the ground like spatters of bright paint. Grass spread around us as far as the eye could see, and I was tempted to lie down and roll in the green softness of it.

"They refused to take an oath of allegiance to the state and get a license from the governor to live here in the territory," she explained, her eyes so filled with sadness I had to turn away. This was what Aunt Sadie had been talking about earlier, but it seemed she neglected to tell me a lot of things I should know.

Puzzled, I shook my head. "Why would they make them do that?"

Callie looked at me without speaking. "Because they want our land," she said finally. "The state wants us to give up our land and move away.

"Why does your father want to go to Milledgeville?" she asked. "Some of the others were sentenced to hard labor there."

Before I could answer, a dog zipped out of nowhere and plowed into Callie's lap, and for a minute I thought of Gulliver and had that awful hollow feeling where my heart's supposed to be.

But, this dog looked nothing like ours. "Go away, Tassel! Go home." Callie laughed as the dog licked her face, golden tail waving like a plume. "He doesn't understand why he's not allowed in the schoolroom," she said, ruffling the dog's coppery coat, "but Miss Sawyer doesn't like it." Laughing, she pointed to the boy racing with Joseph. "Jack brought his pet pig one day and it ran all around the room and under the teacher's desk before he could catch it."

"I wish I could've seen that!" I told her, laughing. I asked her about the two little Negro boys and why they were in school.

Callie seemed puzzled. "Well, they're there to learn

like everybody else. Why?"

I shrugged. "I just thought they were slaves. Slaves don't go to school."

Callie frowned. "They do here. Benjamin is only in his first year but Jacob is one of our better readers and much quicker at sums than I am."

Our teacher came out on the steps and blew the horn to let us know our playtime was over and everyone lined up quietly to go inside.

The afternoon was spent in writing exercises and arithmetic drills and I was glad Miss Mary Rose had made me memorize the multiplication table, although at the time I could think of a million other things I'd rather be doing.

"I have to gather eggs and help with my little sister," Callie said as we hurried from school that afternoon. "Do you think your aunt might allow you to come over later? We can memorize our verses together? It's no fun learning with my brother—Joseph has no patience at all!"

"I'll ask, but I'm sure she won't mind," I said, "if it's all right with your mother."

Callie nodded. "Mother will be spinning today, so as long as we keep an eye on Awinita, she'll be glad to have you there."

"Awinita? Is that your little sister?"

Callie laughed. "Her name means, fawn, and it suits her perfectly. She's two and always jumping around!"

I was glad she hadn't asked about Milledgeville again. If Papa was elected to the legislature, he would be a representative of the state that, according to Callie, wanted to take away their land. Surely that couldn't be true! Calling goodbye to Callie, I ran all the way to my uncle's house, planning to ask Aunt Nancy about it. But I found my aunt walking the floor with a fretful baby.

I looked about, feeling useless. "What can I do?" I asked finally, hoping she'd say she didn't need me.

My aunt shifted the baby to her other shoulder and smiled at me. "It would help if you would prepare the vegetables for supper," she said, directing my attention to the table where a bowl of carrots, potatoes and onions waited to be peeled and sliced.

I had never been allowed to use a knife, but I'd watched our cook Patsy pare apples without breaking the peeling. When you toss it over your left shoulder it's supposed to spell the initial of the man you're going to marry but every time I did it, mine turned out to look like an *L*.

"Lawrence Dupree!" my brother Tom would tease. "You're going to marry Lawrence Dupree and live in a tree!"

Lawrence Dupree went to our church. He had warts all over his hands, his nose ran all the time, and he always sang off key. I couldn't stand him, and of course my brother knew that and tormented me until Lucy made him stop.

I thought I'd never want to hear that silly chant, again—but, oh—I would welcome it now!

"I can try," I said, wishing I had paid more attention to Patsy.

"Or, if you'd rather, you can try your hand with Helen. She has a touch of the colic, but likes to be rocked and sung to."

I was ashamed to tell her I'd never rocked a baby but my friend Lily had a baby brother and I remembered her telling me you had to support the baby's head.

I'll do my best," I said, and held out my arms.

Well, Papa caught a possum in the henhouse once that didn't wiggle and squirm as much as that baby, and I hurried to sit before I dropped her. Inching the rocking chair closer to the fire, I began singing all the nursery rhymes I could remember. Starting with "Here We Go Round the Mulberry Bush," I followed with "London Bridge is Falling Down," "Mary Had a Little Lamb," and "Do You Know the Muffin Man." Baby Helen didn't like any of them. She stuck her legs straight out and screamed until her face turned so red I was afraid it would burst into flame. Aunt Nancy, calmly peeling potatoes, seemed not to notice.

Following her example, I lifted the baby to my shoulder. If she didn't like nursery rhymes, I would just have to try something else. When I was small, Papa taught me to sing the Irish ballad, "My Poor Dog Tray," although my voice was no match for his sweet tenor. I sang it now, and followed it with "Robin Adair."

Helen looked up at me, gray eyes bright with tears, as if she was curious to hear how the song ended. By the time I got to the verse:

What, when the play was o'er, what made my heart so sore,
Oh, it was parting with Robin Adair . . .

She was asleep.

Aunt Nancy blinked away onion tears and smiled at me. "Why, that was lovely, Nell. I believe you've worked a bit of magic here."

I smiled my thanks and carefully laid the sleeping baby in her cradle. Thank goodness I was good for something!

Chapter Six

I slid onto the bench beside my aunt and watched her peel carrots with quick strokes of the knife. I wanted to ask her if Callie was right about the state planning to take Cherokee land, but I wasn't sure I wanted to hear the answer.

She slipped the vegetables into a pot simmering over the fire and wiped her hands on her apron. "Tell me about your first day at school," she said, smiling. "I hope everything went well."

"It was different," I admitted, "but I made a new friend." And I told her about Callie. "She invited me to come over so we can memorize our scriptures together."

"I think that's a fine idea! Callie's close to your age and her mother is a friend of mine, but don't stay too long. The days are getting shorter and it'll be dark before we know it."

I nodded, but hesitated to leave. "Aunt Nancy," I asked finally, "is it true that the state wants the Cherokees to give up their land?"

Sighing, she put both hands on the table and stared down at it as if memorizing the grain of the wood, and when she looked up at me her eyes had kind of a lost look. "Yes, Nell, I'm afraid it is true. I'm sorry you had to hear it like that, but it's too late to pretend anymore.

Naturally it has been discussed at school, and I'm sure you heard that your uncle John was imprisoned for a while, along with others." Sitting beside me, she reached for my hand. "The government gave this land to the Cherokees, and now they've decided they want it back. The tribes are not even allowed to govern themselves now or to have council meetings. Just last month they had to meet in Alabama because of that. Your uncle John, and others who think the same way, didn't consider it just to take an oath of allegiance to the state when this is supposed to be Cherokee Territory."

"Then why did he?" I asked.

"He would've had to serve four years at hard labor, Nell. Little Helen was on the way, and he has a family to care for. He had no choice." She rose to stir the pot over the fire. "Too, he can do more good right here in the print shop than locked away at the capital in Milledgeville."

I thought of the children I'd met that day at the Council House, of their peaceful green village where two great rivers meet to become the wide Oostanaula. What would become of it then? Of them?

I stood to warm myself by the fire. "What's going to happen now?"

"I don't believe anything will come of it soon. At least I hope it won't." My aunt swung the pot away from the flames and placed a hand on my shoulder. "Chief John Ross will do his best to convince the people in Washington of our right to remain. He won't give up easily."

It was hard to tell if she believed what she was saying or was just trying to put me at ease. I'd heard grown-ups talk that way before.

"If you're going to Callie's," my aunt reminded me, "I suppose you'd best go on, but don't stay too long."

Tassel came to greet me as I approached Callie's cabin and as I drew closer, I heard the sound of someone chopping wood. Joseph laid the ax aside to gather an armload of firewood so I held the door open for him and was rewarded with a mumbled thank you. Callie seemed glad to see me and led me inside. "I was afraid you weren't coming," she said. "Let's sit by the fire where it's warm to memorize our verses.

"This is my sister, Awinita," she said, nodding to a little girl who was attempting to dress a rag doll in a dress that was much too large. "Don't try to help," she whispered. "She likes to do it herself."

I told Awinita I liked her doll, although it was hard to tell what it looked like since it seemed swallowed in the dress, and Callie laughed. "Your aunt made her the doll, and Awinita wore that dress as a baby so she thinks her doll should wear it too."

Other than Aunt Nancy's, I had never been in a Cherokee home before and was surprised to see it wasn't much different from some I'd seen in Athens. The large room had puncheon floors with bright rugs scattered about. A rocking chair waited in front of the fire and the table was laid with dishes and tableware much like the kind we used at home. Callie introduced her mother who looked up and smiled from her spinning wheel on the other side of the room. A candle burned on the table beside her and another on the mantel. A ladder on the other end of the long room led to a loft, and glass-paned windows on either side of the door let in light.

"Your mother's pretty," I whispered aside to Callie and she nodded and smiled. I could tell she thought so too. She stooped to stir something that looked like oatmeal in a pot over the coals. Callie called it canuchi and explained it was a mush made of crushed hickory nuts and corn meal. The rich smell of sweet potatoes baking in a Dutch oven reminded me it would soon be time to eat.

For the first time I noticed the beaded jewelry she wore around her neck. "Your necklace is pretty," I told her. "Did you make it yourself?"

Smiling, she fingered it as she spoke. "My grandmother made this for my mother, and she passed it along to me. The crow brings wisdom and helps us to face new challenges, and the feather represents honor and strength."

The beaded design, in bright colors of blue, orange, yellow, and black, showed the image of a crow holding a feather in his beak, and I couldn't blame her for being proud of it. I wished someone would make one for me.

Our teacher had assigned us the first ten verses of the third chapter of Acts. I had heard them often at home and in church and found comfort in the rhythm of the words as well as their meaning. We took time about reciting them to each other until we felt we knew them well, but I could see it was getting darker outside. I was getting ready to leave when Callie's father arrived.

He wore a turban of bright calico and was so tall he had to stoop a bit to come inside. His skin was the ruddy color of river bank clay.

"This is my father," Callie said, rising to meet him. He reminded me of the kind Indian who had helped get our wagon out of the rut and I smiled and said hello.

He nodded and barely mumbled a greeting, or I suppose it was a greeting. It was difficult to say. Joseph had disappeared earlier into the loft, so I said goodbye to Callie and her family and hurried away, thinking it was easy to know where Joseph had inherited his sullen personality.

The next day Callie and I were rewarded with bright beaded hair ornaments for learning our bible verses. I thought they were pretty and wondered who had made them. Maybe Miss Sawyer . . . but probably not.

After Scripture reading, Miss Sawyer pointed out Greece to us on the globe she had bought for our classroom, and after she told us about the poverty there, my classmates decided to collect money for the poor children in that country. When students brought in their contributions the next day we had a total of three dollars and sixty cents to send to the American Board.

Little Will became so discouraged with his reading lesson that morning I was afraid he was going to cry. How could we expect him to read English when he could hardly speak it?

"Why not teach him first in Cherokee?" Callie suggested. "If he learns to read using the syllabary Sequoyah gave us, it might make it easier for him to understand."

Many of my classmates, including Callie and her brother, could read and speak in the Cherokee language, and our teacher agreed this might be a good beginning for Little Will.

Sequoyah's alphabet was not really an alphabet but a

syllabus made up of eighty-five common syllables used in the Cherokee language. Since I didn't speak the language, it held no meaning for me, but Callie, as well as many in the class, could read it easily. For the next few days, she and Joseph and several others took time working with him until gradually Little Will began to understand and read with ease the simple exercises our teacher had written for him.

I hadn't told anyone, even Aunt Nancy, about my reaction to Callie's father. Many of the Cherokees dressed differently and practiced customs foreign to me, and I had come to expect that. But Callie's father . . . well . . . he made me feel afraid. And for a while, he was the only one until I met the old woman at the spring.

Kate had stopped by after school that day and Aunt Nancy took advantage of her visit to send the two of us to fill buckets from the spring. The woman didn't seem to notice us when we came upon her kneeling there. Her long gray hair hung in strands about her face and she wore a skirt of rabbit skins sewn together that came just below her knees. I spoke to her, as it was the polite thing to do, and she looked up at me and said something in Cherokee I couldn't understand.

"I'm sorry," I said, and smiled, ignoring Kate's tug on my arm, then stumbled aside when the rude woman gathered up her pot and pushed past us. She seemed not to notice the freezing water she sloshed on us as she passed.

"Who was *that*? I asked, feeling liked I'd swallowed an icicle whole.

Kate's laugh was kind of shaky. "I tried to warn

you. That's Inola, the medicine woman. She's a little different."

"Different? She looks like a witch!"

Kate stooped to fill her bucket. "There are some who think she is, but Papa says she knows more about medicine than most doctors."

"I wouldn't want her to doctor me!" I said. And shuddered.

But before the week was out, I would have to seek her help.

Chapter Seven

"The baby feels a little warm," Uncle John said. "Do you think she's coming down with a fever?"

Aunt Nancy laid her needlework aside and rested her hand on Helen's forehead. "She seems all right to me, and there's nothing wrong with her appetite. It's probably because you're sitting so close to the fire."

I had soon learned my uncle didn't have a lot to say. He worked hard in the print shop all day, and with Mr. Boudinot away, probably had more duties than usual, although he never said so, but he always took time to talk with me and ask about my day. And he adored little Helen. As soon as the evening meal was over, it wasn't unusual for him to hold her until bedtime.

The baby was fretful during the night but seemed to be fine the next morning and went right to sleep after nursing, so Uncle John left reluctantly for Knoxville to order printing supplies. Since Samuel Worcester, the postmaster at New Echota, was still in prison in Milledgeville, my uncle explained, they weren't receiving deliveries for *The Phoenix* as they should.

After a cold, dreary morning, the day warmed by afternoon, and by the time we were dismissed from school, the town was washed in sunshine; yet in spite of it, I felt empty and sad.

"Is something troubling you? You aren't ill, are

you?" Callie asked as we left the Council House together.

She looked so sad with her soft brown eyes mir-
roring my dark mood I didn't answer right away because
I was afraid it would hurt her feelings. I knew very well
what was wrong with me—I was homesick. I had been
at New Echota for a little over two weeks and had yet
to receive a letter from home.

Didn't Papa care about me any more? Why didn't
he write? After all, it was his leg that was broken, not his
hand. And then I began to feel sorry for thinking such a
thing. What if Papa had taken a turn for the worse? I
had heard of people who developed complications from
a broken bone. He might even—well, I wasn't going to
think of that! Besides, I reasoned, my brother would let
me know. Wouldn't he?

For a minute Callie stood silently fingering her
necklace of colorful carved beads. "If Mother doesn't
need my help, after I gather the eggs, I'll take you to my
secret place."

She had a big, wide smile on her face, so it was impossible not to smile back. "I didn't know you had a
secret place," I said.

Callie laughed. "That's because it's a secret!"

I guess I thought I was the only one with a secret
place. Mine was underneath the grape arbor behind the
wash house at home and I liked to pretend nobody
knew about it but me, but I kind of suspected they did.

Uncle John had killed and skinned a rabbit the day
before and I could smell the stew simmering over the
fire as soon as I stepped inside. Aunt Nancy looked up
from nursing Helen and greeted me. She seemed worried in spite of her smile and I asked about the baby.

"Not as hungry as usual. I'm afraid she might be coming down with a cold."

I asked if I could help and was relieved when she asked only that I bring her a few apples from the shed behind the house. Aunt Nancy stored potatoes, onions, cabbage and squash in there, as well as a barrel of apples from the trees in the orchard. Most had been dried earlier but these were used for eating, applesauce and baking.

"Run along and enjoy the sunshine while it lasts," she told me when I returned, "but don't wander too far. It's getting darker much earlier now."

I promised I wouldn't and hurried outside where Callie waited for me, impatient to be off.

"Where are we going?" I asked as we reached the end of the village street. I was almost out of breath trying to keep up with her.

Callie bit into the apple I'd brought her. "It's on the way to Mr. Worcester's house—kind of a long way, so we'll have to hurry."

Once we cleared the village, the few houses we saw were set back from the road. We passed a large green area where cattle grazed behind a split rail fence and squawking chickens scattered about the doorstep of a small cabin. A few pigs roamed under the bare trees of an apple orchard on the other side of the road.

"Listen!" Callie stopped suddenly, throwing out an arm in front of me.

I stood still as a slight wind ruffled my bonnet. "What? I don't hear anything."

"It's the wind . . . it's singing in the cornfield. Don't you hear it?"

I laughed. "What's it singing?"

I thought she was joking, but Callie stood, eyes closed and didn't speak for a minute. "It's singing of the harvest, of the winter to come. It's singing of the people who lived here before us, of the animals who roamed the land."

Maybe if I closed my eyes, I thought. And so I did. *Dry leaves, wood smoke, fodder that reminded me of Liberty's stall in the stable back home. The peaceful music of corn stalks rustling in the wind.* It was singing a lullaby.

The trees grew denser after we crossed a bridge over a small stream and Callie hesitated and looked about.

"Is it much farther?" I wanted to know.

Frowning, she seemed to be examining a narrow trail that led into a dark wooded area. "We're almost there," she assured me, "but do you see that path over there? That's where Inola lives. Her cabin's in the bend of the creek but you can't see it from here."

"Well, that suits me fine!" I said. Suddenly it seemed to be getting darker. "Where *is* this secret place?"

"I would never have found it if Tassel hadn't been chasing a rabbit." Callie raced ahead, pushing her way through a thicket of undergrowth. "It's back a little way, but I know where to look because there's a big rock right before you leave the trail."

I stumbled after her, skirting pine saplings and untangling myself from muscadine vines, bare now, but recently heavy with dark pungent grapes, and for a minute I lost sight of her. The rustling scurry of footsteps through layers of dried leaves led me to a secluded open area not much larger than my uncle's smokehouse. Grass as green as summer carpeted the ground that had been swept clear, and in it center was the strangest tree I had ever seen.

I knew it was an oak because a few brown leaves and acorns were scattered around its base. About three or four feet from the ground a limb of the tree grew at a right angle from the trunk making a perfect place to sit.

"Come on!" Callie swung herself onto the limb and made room for me to join her.

I did. "What made it grow like this?" I asked. "I've never seen anything like it."

Callie's long skirt swished as she swung her feet. "It's a trail marker tree," she said. "It was made to grow this way to show a direction, or maybe let travelers know there was water nearby."

"How did they do that?"

Callie pointed out deep scars on the tree where it had been made to bend from the trunk by tying it down, and another in the place where it curved upward. Another method, she said, was to create a thong by using a small sapling to force it. A peculiar bulging knot where the tree bent upward was called a nose, Callie explained, and was created by inserting charred wood from the same tree under the bark. The purpose of this was to let travelers know which direction to take.

"I wonder who made it like this," I said.

"Some of our early ancestors," Callie told me. "The Cherokee have been here a long, long time." She smiled. "Might even have been one of mine."

If there had been a trail in the direction the nose seemed to be pointing, it had long since disappeared.

"Wait until you see this place in the spring," Callie said. "The ground is covered in flowers: white ones so tiny you can hardly see them, and a lot of yellow ones—

like daisies, only smaller, sprinkled over the grass. But the pink one is my favorite. It looks like a teardrop on a long stem. I dug up a few and brought them home for Mother to plant in her garden, and I can't wait to see if they come up in the spring. If we're still here then," she added, speaking softly to herself.

My friend's secret place was beautiful even in November and I could see why it was special to her. "It must look like a fairyland," I said.

"And there are trees, too—trees with pretty white flowers—not just here, but all around," she said.

A chill wind rustled through the woods surrounding us and I wished I had thought to bring a shawl. Shadows crept over the grass that had been bright before and the sky had turned to gray.

"I promised my aunt I wouldn't be late," I said, jumping from my perch.

Following me, Callie sighed. "When I'm here, it's hard to remember any place else."

I was hungry for the rabbit stew and corn cakes my aunt had ready for supper but noticed she didn't eat much of hers. Baby Helen had shown little interest in nursing, she told me, but had finally fallen asleep. After eating, I cleared away the few dishes and washed them, wishing I could do more to help. Later, Aunt Nancy brought out the fabric for a shirt she was making for my uncle's Christmas gift. It was a fine white linen she had ordered from Elijah Hicks' store and was to be a surprise. Her fingers worked quickly drawing the needle in and out of the cloth and I doubted if I would ever be able to sew with such tiny stitches.

As we sat by the fire I told her about the trail mark-er tree I had seen, but of course I didn't tell her where it was. After all, it *was* a secret place.

I was surprised to learn my aunt knew all about it. "Once in a while we still come upon those, but they're fast disappearing. Years ago that must've marked a trail through here," she said. "Our people have lived in this area for many years."

Later, as I lay in bed, I thought about her words. The Cherokee had lived in this country long before the white settlers came, and now our government wanted to take their land. Aunt Sadie had led me to believe that if Papa had been elected to the state legislature, he would be sympathetic to the Cherokee cause. If his leg healed quickly, I thought, maybe it wouldn't be too late. It seemed to me they needed all the help they could get.

I had just fallen asleep when Lucy called for me to get up. Was it already time to get dressed and go downstairs for breakfast?

But it wasn't Lucy, and I wasn't in my bed back in Athens. I opened my eyes to darkness and saw my aunt standing beside my bed with a candle.

"The baby is very sick, and I can't leave her. You're going to have to go for help." My aunt's voice, usually calm and strong, was heavy with fear.

I threw aside the covers and groped in the darkness for shoes and clothing, wishing I could shut out the sound of Helen's labored breathing. Tiny and helpless, she lay in her cradle by the fire, too sick to even cry, and I wanted to scoop her up and kiss her hurt away. It wasn't unusual for babies to die, and I knew of many families who had lost one or more to illnesses our doctors didn't know how to cure. Callie had told me that just last summer the missionary, Samuel Worchester, and his wife had lost a baby girl.

But our baby couldn't die! *Oh, please, God, don't let her die!* "Of course I'll help!" I looked up into Aunt Nancy's frantic face and my heart beat so hard and so fast it hurt my chest. I wanted to cover my face and cry, but what good would my crying do? "Just tell me where to go," I said. I seemed to have ten fingers on each hand and it was taking me forever just to put on my boots.

"Nell, if there was anyone else—" My aunt reached out to me and I grasped her hand. "John and my brother are both away, and I can't ask his wife to leave her little ones . . ." She lit an oil lantern with the flame from her candle and set it on the table. "It's not an easy place to find, so listen carefully and I'll tell you how to get there."

I nodded. "Where am I going?"

"You have to get Inola, and tell her Helen's having trouble breathing. Tell her to hurry!"

"Inola? Isn't she the—"

"The medicine woman—yes. She'll know what to do. She's the only one who can help us."

"I know how to find her," I said, and hoped my voice didn't give my doubt away. Could I find that path in the dark? "Callie showed me where she lives."

Aunt Nancy draped a length of woolen cloth over my head and tucked it under my chin, then wrapped my cape around me before handing me the lantern. "The moonlight should help some, but once you get into the trees, you're going to have to be very careful. Watch where you step and hold the lantern steady."

She stood in the doorway watching as I left, my lantern casting a pool of yellow light around me. It was easy making my way down the wide street. I walked past dark buildings silhouetted in the moonlight, skeleton trees stretching arms to the sky. I remembered that Callie had pointed out the path to Inola's place just after we crossed a bridge and hoped I would be able to see it in the dark.

The way narrowed as trees closed around me and I slowed my pace to be sure of the road at my feet. My fear of the dark unknown was replaced by something worse—I wouldn't find her in time.

Chapter Eight

I remembered Callie pointing out the path to the medicine woman's house soon after we crossed the bridge and wished I had paid closer attention. If only Callie were with me now! Holding the lantern higher, I walked carefully over the bridge and stopped to look around. Except for the dim yellow circle of light, I was surrounded by darkness . . . and silence. If I reached the stone on the left that marked the turn to Callie's secret place, I would've gone too far. The constant flutter in my chest urged me to hurry, but how many times had Miss Mary Rose reminded me of the quote from Benjamin Franklin: *Haste makes waste?* I didn't have time to make mistakes.

A sudden wind sent dry leaves scuttling in front of me and I stepped cautiously onto what I hoped was the path to Inola's and help. But what if it wasn't? What if I wandered deeper into the woods and couldn't find my way out?

I jumped, making the lantern swing wildly when a tree limb cracked and fell with a crash not far away. If there was a house up ahead I couldn't see it, but as frightened as I was of confronting the medicine woman, she couldn't be scarier than the sickness that threatened my tiny cousin.

Surely I should've reached the place by now. Underbrush clawed at my clothing and I was about to turn and try to find my way back to the main road when the woman appeared suddenly in front of me. She looked like something from a nightmare and I would have turned and run if my feet—or, not just my feet, but all of me—hadn't frozen in place.

I waited for her to pounce on me or at least to yell, but she seemed to be waiting for me to speak.

"It's the baby—Aunt Nancy's baby!" My voice came out in a quivering squeak. "She can't breathe! Come—please come!"

"You go! Tell her I come!" With one hand she gave me a shove that jolted me out of my terrified trance and I started to run.

"You hurry!" she shouted after me. But I was already on my way.

My aunt met me in the doorway with Helen in her arms, and her face told me the baby's condition hadn't improved.

"She's on the way," I told her, and she laid a gentle hand on my shoulder in silent thanks.

I was surprised when the medicine woman arrived soon after as I had run all the way. Setting her lantern on the table, she took the baby from her mother's arms, stripped away its clothing, and laid her on a blanket before the fire where she moved her hands over Helen's little body, chanting all the while. Speaking in Cherokee, she began to give directions to my aunt. I couldn't understand what she said, but Aunt Nancy filled the cast iron pot with water and swung it over the fire. When the water began to boil, Inola dipped some into a cup and threw in a dried grayish plant my aunt said was an herb called boneset.

Inola's big shell earrings swung about as she shook a colorful gourd over the baby. While the brew was steeping, she said something to my aunt who, silently taking a lantern, motioned for me to come with her. Stepping outside, she instructed me to help her break off twigs from a white pine sapling at the edge of the yard. After gathering some in our aprons, my aunt threw them into a pot of steaming water and they filled the room with their fresh green smell.

The medicine woman strained the boneset brew through a piece of cloth and muttered something I didn't understand.

"Honey," my aunt explained, taking a jar from the cupboard. "She wants it to sweeten the tea."

Then, while holding the baby in her arms, Inola dipped a small piece of fabric in the tea and let the cooling liquid dribble slowly into Helen's mouth.

"She's choking!" I cried out in protest when the baby sputtered and turned her head away. But Aunt Nancy shook her head. "She just got a bit too much, Nell. She's not accustomed to taking liquids this way."

"The tea? What is it for?" I asked as Inola tried again, this time with only a few drops at a time.

"It's to bring down the fever and help her breathe better," she said, and wrapping Helen in a light cover, laid her in her cradle closer to the pine-scented steam. "We'll keep giving her small doses for as long as we can get her to take them."

Squatting beside us, Inola took a small brown bundle from the strange bag she carried and began to mix a portion of the contents with some of the water from the pot. This she spread on a warm cloth which she folded over and placed on the baby's chest. It had a fresh, woodsy scent and my aunt explained it was a poultice made from the inner bark of the white pine. "It's to ease her breathing," she said. "And when that cools, we'll replace it with more."

Helen's breathing was still strained and her small body flushed with fever. I could hardly bear to look at her without crying so I stared at the flames leaping about in the fireplace until they almost put me in a trance.

"You should get some sleep, Nell," my aunt advised me. "There's really nothing more you can do tonight."

But what might happen if I left the room? I curled beside the fire and fought to keep my eyes from closing.

But of course they did. I woke at one point during the night to see my aunt walking about the room with the baby on her shoulder singing a song with words I did not know while the medicine woman squatted to add pine twigs to the steaming pot.

The gray light of early morning streaked across the cabin floor when I woke again and threw off the cover my aunt had placed over me.

The room was filled with the scent of pine, and a charred log fell in the fireplace sending embers up the chimney. It took only a few seconds for me to come to terms with the silence. No soothing lullaby. No muttered voices. *No rasping breathing.*

A knife-like pain cut through my middle and I couldn't get my breath. I didn't want to look. If I didn't look, I wouldn't know, and I didn't want to know. Inola was gone and my aunt slept curled in a chair beside a silent cradle.

"Nell?" Aunt Nancy sat up and held out her arms to me, and she smiled. *Smiled!*

"The baby's fever broke early this morning and her breathing has eased." Still clutching my hand, she fell to her knees. "Thanks be to God!"

And to Inola, I thought, but I fell to my knees, too, since she hadn't let go of my hand. Papa had explained to me that my uncle John had married into a Cherokee family that had been educated by Protestant missionaries in Tennessee and Georgia, and her brother, Elias Boudinot, had even studied at Andover Theological School while in Connecticut.

I was thankful to see the feverish flush gone from little Helen's face and the sound of her breathing no longer frightened me as it had. The baby would be frail, and probably fretful, for a while, and we would have to watch her carefully, my aunt said.

I touched her tiny fist as she waved it about and her fingers closed around mine. I would watch her as long as needed. It was hard to believe that a little over a month ago I wouldn't have thought it possible to ache like this.

Chapter Nine

For a minute I thought I was back in Athens in Aunt Ida's front parlor.

I had hurried from school clutching my cape about me while the mean November wind billowed my skirts and sent brown leaves swirling. Maybe my aunt would have some of her spicy apple cider simmering over the fire. Although it was only a short walk from the Council House, I felt cold through and through and was eager to get warm. Aunt Nancy hadn't let the fire burn low since baby Helen's illness a few days before and now spent more time rocking her as if she was afraid to put her down. I didn't blame her.

But today the baby slept quietly in her cradle while my aunt and another woman spoke in low voices and sipped from familiar china cups.

Aunt Nancy greeted me with a smile. "Nell, come and meet our neighbor, Mrs. Boudinot. Her husband, Elias, is editor of our paper, *The Phoenix*."

I had been told Mr. Boudinot had married a lady he met while in school in Connecticut and somehow assumed his wife was Cherokee. I'm afraid my surprise must have been obvious on learning she was white, although I clumsily tried to hide it.

She was small with a narrow face and dark eyes that shone with warmth as she extended a hand hardly larger than my own. "Welcome to our little community, Nell. I understand you're attending school with some of our young students.

"My goodness! Your hand is freezing. Come and get warm by the fire," she said, drawing me closer.

Glad for the invitation, I quickly complied. "Do you have children in school here?" I asked, and she shook her head and laughed. "Not yet, but I hope some day they will be. Eleanor and Mary are still small and little Cornelius isn't much bigger than your cousin Helen."

I glanced at the sleeping baby. "Is she still coughing?" I asked my aunt.

"Not nearly as much, and sleeping better, too. I expect she'll be hungry soon . . . and look at the sweet dress Harriett—Mrs. Boudinot—brought her," she said, calling my attention to the small garment in her lap.

"Our Eleanor and Mary both wore this," our neighbor said, "but I don't think it's suitable for a little boy." Setting her teacup aside, she turned to me. "My Christian name is Harriett, Nell, but my Cherokee friends call me Kalahdee."

Having been raised in New England, her speech was different from ours but

I found it to be friendly and pleasing. "Is it all right if I call you Miss Harriett?" *What would Papa think if I addressed a grown lady by her first name only?*

"Our friend brought another surprise," my aunt told me, "and this one's for you, Nell."

Harriett Boudinot nodded. "I collected our mail from the post office this morning and noticed a letter had arrived for you."

Aunt Nancy smiled. "You'll find it on your bed, and I think it's the one you've been looking for."

"Is it from Papa?"

Oh, please let it be from Papa! I raced to my tiny alcove room and snatched up the folded letter addressed to me in Papa's familiar handwriting. Sitting on the bed, I made myself wait to open it until my hands stopped trembling for fear I would tear the fragile paper. I had never received a letter before—or at least one that was addressed just to me, and I ran my fingers lovingly over the lines my father had written and read it through my tears.

My Dear Daughter,

Not a day goes by that I don't think of you and hope you are well. The house seems empty without you and we look forward to the day when I can bring you home again. I think Lucy misses you as much as I do and sends her love, as does your Aunt Ida.

My leg feels stronger every day, although I don't think I'll be dancing a jig any time soon. Dr. Means seems pleased with my recovery thus far but reminds me I still have a way to go. With help, by Christmas I hope to be able to take a few steps.

Your brother is doing well in his studies at the College and said he looks forward to challenging you to a game of checkers on your return.

Poor Gulliver keeps looking for you all over the house and Lucy tells me he still sleeps by your bed every night.

I hope you are learning a lot in school there and are being a help to your Aunt Nancy.

Since you'll be unable to spend Christmas with us, look for a little bit of home to arrive before long.

Sending my best to Nancy and John and a kiss

for Baby Helen.

Your loving Papa

I had begun to cry by the first paragraph and by the time I got to the part about Gulliver, I could've probably filled a milk pail with my tears—partly in relief that Papa was getting better, but mostly because I missed them so.

In less than a week it would be December and in our little Methodist Church back in Athens, the congregation would soon begin singing my favorite hymns like "Joy to the World," and "The First Noel," and on Christmas Eve, some of the women would decorate the church with holly and fragrant branches of cedar and pine. Services at New Echota were held in the Council House which we used for school on weekdays. I hoped they would follow that custom here.

Would I have time to make something for Papa and Lucy in time for Christmas? Maybe Aunt Nancy would help me. Carefully refolding my letter, I laid it on the little table by my bed and hurried to rejoin the two by the fire.

"I don't suppose you've had word from my brother," my aunt was saying.

Mrs. Boudinot shook her head. "I was hoping for a letter this morning, but I fear he might be waiting until he has better news. As you know, paper, ink, and other supplies have to be shipped from Savannah or Knoxville, and this adds to the expense. If we don't find more financial help to keep the *Phoenix* in circulation, I don't know how we're going to continue."

"I'm afraid people are reluctant to make a commitment because of the president's plan of removal." The

baby began to stir and Aunt Nancy picked her up gently, patted her, and held her close. "I'm hoping . . . we're
all hoping that won't come to pass, but it seems
President Jackson is determined to take our land—especially since gold has been discovered in the eastern part
of the Nation."

Harriett Boudinot spoke in a voice so low I could
hardly hear her. "On *Cherokee* land . . . it's not right,
Nancy. It's hard to believe there's such greed. I'm pray-
ing Chief Ross can settle this peacefully. I understand he
plans to take a delegation to Washington."

Aunt Nancy sighed. "I suppose we'll just have to
have faith."

Mrs. Boudinot stared into the fireplace as a charred
log disintegrated into ashes. "And courage," she said
finally.

"And Ann . . . how is she? That poor woman seems
to have more than her share," my aunt said, and I supposed she was speaking of Ann Worcester who, with
her two children, was living with the Boudinots while
her missionary husband was being held in Milledgeville.

"Still frail, but she seems much stronger now. As
you know, Ann was ill even before their baby died. But
she tries to keep up her spirits for the children, and, I
expect, for the sake of her husband as well. I'm sure Mr.
Weaver has told you that with her help they've been
able to print three thousand copies of the second edition of the Gospel of Matthew, and another edition of
the *Hymn Book.*

Ann Worcester and Dr. Butler's wife had recently
returned from a visit to their husbands in prison where
they were able to provide them with blankets and other
comforts. The two women were pleased to find both

men cheerful and busy, as well as loved and respected.

Aunt Nancy smiled. "I think that visit did Mrs. Worcester more good than any medicine. From what I hear, both her husband and Dr. Butler are trying their best to be cheerful under the circumstances. At least they're staying busy. Mr. Worcester conducts Sabbath services for the prisoners in addition to working as a carpenter and blacksmith, and Dr. Butler is turning a lathe wheel."

Harriett Boudinot shook her head. "Well, they've applied to the United States Supreme Court and expect a hearing in the winter. Let's just hope the decision will be in their favor."

The two women hadn't noticed me standing there and I hesitated to call attention to myself as I listened to what they were saying. Worrying about Christmas gifts didn't seem so important now.

Chapter Ten

"You want to do *what?*"

Callie was nurturing a secret and I had tried all day to get her to tell me what it was until I finally wore her down.

She fingered her beaded necklace, a habit of hers I'd noticed when she seemed unsure of something. "Not so loud!" she whispered. "Do you want everybody to hear?"

It was an unusually mild day in early December and we took our time after school getting water at the spring. My aunt wanted to get an early start on her washing the next morning and each pail full would be added to the big hollowed oak log used to store it.

My friend looked around to be sure no one was in hearing distance. "I want to shoot stalks," she said.

I thought about that for a minute while icy water sloshed onto my foot. "Why?" I asked.

Callie didn't answer right away but just looked at me kind of funny. "It's a game—a competition," she explained. "Teams come here from Pine Log, sometimes Oothcaloga—all around, and it's played on a big field . . ." She sighed. "Come on, I'll show you."

After emptying our pails in Aunt Nancy's waist-high log, Callie raced ahead of me past Mr. McCoy's tavern and the Council House. By the time we reached the stone house at the edge of the village where Lewis Ross and his wife Lavender lived, I was out of breath from trying to keep up. Callie, who didn't seem to be winded at all, waited impatiently in an open field.

"There will be stacks of corn stalks at both ends," she explained, throwing her out her arms. "They're bound together to make a target about three feet high and three feet wide.

"Each shooter tries to make his arrow pierce as many stalks as he can," she added, noticing my puzzled expression. "Four poles will make kind of a rack tied across the top to keep the stalks in place," Callie explained. "Each stalk the arrow pierces counts as a point, and the shooter who reaches fifty points first is the winner."

"Can you do that?" I asked. "Shoot with a bow?"

Callie nodded, her eyes shining. "Papa made my bow himself from wood from the Osage orange tree, and my arrows are made of black locust. "Those are the best—at least, Papa says they are.

"The stalk shooting's in a few days," she added. "It takes that long to get the stalks ready and for the other teams to get here. "Some of the team from Pine Log are already here, and Mother and the other women will be busy cooking for everybody but . . ." Callie lowered her voice. "I'm going to ask if I can try for the team."

Frowning, I glanced behind us. "Why are you whispering?"

"Shh! I thought I heard something. Somebody must have followed us."

Well, that was a scary thought. There wasn't much daylight left and the surrounding woods seemed to be closing in around us. "Aren't we supposed to be here?"

I asked, preparing to lift up my skirts and run.

Callie made a face. "It's just that—"

"Only *men* are allowed to compete in stalk shooting!" Scowling, Callie's brother Joseph stood at the edge of the woods behind us, feet apart, arms folded, as if he dared us to challenge him.

Ignoring him, Callie turned to me. "Don't pay any attention to him! He's jealous because he knows I'm a better shot."

Her brother laughed. "Too bad you won't be able to prove it since you won't be taking part."

"Is that true?" I asked Callie. "Are only men allowed to compete?"

Callie shrugged. "That's the way its always been, but I'm going to ask if I can't try this year. Papa knows I can shoot—he taught me himself."

"It's against the rules." Waving his hand in dismissal, Joseph turned to leave. "You'll just be wasting your time."

I could tell by the look on Callie's face that she suspected he was telling the truth and was trying her best not to show her disappointment. She didn't speak as we walked back home in the fading light, and I felt her hurt as if it were mine.

"If you can't take part in the competition, why not have your own?" I said.

She stopped suddenly and looked at me. "What do you mean?"

"Challenge him," I said, "to a contest . . . just between the two of you."

Callie shook her head and frowned. "It's no use . . ." and then she laughed . . . "*unless* there's a chance I can try *before* the shooting begins. "They'll soon be getting the stalks in place to be ready for the shooting the next day."

"But if you aren't supposed to take part . . . won't somebody see you?" I didn't want my friend to get in trouble just to prove a point.

"Not if I get there in the first light before everyone's awake."

"Maybe you won't have to. Wait and see what your papa says," I suggested.

"I'll try to ask him tonight," Callie said. But she didn't seem happy about it.

When I saw my friend's glum face at school the next day I didn't have to ask about the stalk shooting competition. Miss Sawyer didn't waste any time getting started so we didn't have a chance to talk until our noontime break.

The day had turned colder and it seemed to be taking a long time for the room to warm in spite of the number of logs on the fire. Little Will had brought from home a potato baked in the ashes and wrapped in a piece of cloth to keep his hands warm and I wish I'd thought of it, although by the time we finished reading a story from the *Blue Back Speller* he complained the potato had lost its heat.

Because of the weather, Miss Sawyer permitted us to remain inside during the noontime break, and that suited me just fine as my feet were so cold I could hardly feel my toes in spite of my boots and warm wool stockings.

But Callie had other ideas. "Let's go," she whispered, giving my shoulder a poke on her way to the door. Reluctantly, I grabbed my lunch pail, pulled my cape about me and followed.

Frost was still heavy on the ground and the two of us tramped over glistening grass on our way to our usual spot under the maple tree, now bare of leaves.

"It's freezing out here, Callie! Let's go back inside." I'd forgotten to put on my gloves and I set my lunch pail on the ground and buried my hands beneath my cape.

Frowning, she shook her head, keeping an eye on the door behind us. "We can't talk in there. Someone might hear."

I shivered, thinking it would be much easier to talk when you weren't stamping your feet to keep warm, but it was obvious that Callie had something important on her mind and I had a good idea what it was.

"What did your papa say—about the stack shoot?" I asked.

Callie made a face, waving her hand in dismissal. "Same thing Joseph said. It's against the rules!"

"Well, just try again next year," I suggested. "Maybe things will change."

Callie turned away. "Nell, I don't know if we'll even *be here* next year."

"Why can't they change those rules then? Who makes the rules, anyway?"

And for the first time that day Callie laughed. "Why, men do, of course!" She dropped her voice, although there weren't any others around. "Now, here's what I want to do, but I'll need your help."

Huddled beside the maple tree we shared our lunch-es of corn cakes, cheese, and one of Aunt Nancy's fried apple pies while Callie told of her plan. The stalk shooting was to take place in three days time, she told me. Already we had noticed men arriving from Pine Log, Coosawattee and other nearby areas and she had heard her father say the stalks were to be set up the day before the shooting would begin.

"If I were to be there early that morning at first light before time for the shooting to start, I might have a chance at a try," Callie said.

"But what if someone sees you?" I was proud of my friend for her courage but I didn't want her to be in trouble.

"That's where you can help," she told me. "It shouldn't take much time for me to shoot a couple of arrows—just to see how many stalks I can pierce. I'm sure I can do as well—or better—than Joseph, but I'll need you to be my lookout so you can warn me if you hear anyone coming."

I promised that I would, feeling more than a little tingle of excitement at being a part of something so daring.

I told my aunt and uncle I had to leave early the morning of the stalk shooting to work with Callie on a project and hoped they wouldn't mention it to Callie's mother or ask what the project was about. They didn't. They were both too busy getting ready for the competition. I knew Aunt Nancy planned to leave baby Helen with Mrs. Boudinot for several hours so she could help other women with the cooking that day.

It was dark when I left the house that morning but at least it wasn't raining or snowing. There was no school that day as everyone would be watching the shooters so I hurried to our pre-arranged meeting place at the edge of the woods that bordered the field where the stacks were already in place.

New Echota is in a river valley where the Coosawatee meets the Conasauga to form the Oostanaula and a dense fog covered the ground reminding me of graveyards and scary ghost stories. It seemed I waited hours before Callie finally arrived, and to keep from being afraid I pretended the trees behind me were dark sentries there to protect me from anyone who meant me harm. Still, every time a limb creaked or a rabbit scurried through the underbrush I think I swallowed my breath.

"Nell?"

I stepped cautiously from my hiding place behind a pine sapling when Callie called my name. I hadn't heard her approaching.

"I got away as fast as I could. Had to help dress Awinita. Mother's taking her to Mrs. Boudinot's for a while so she can help with the food."

I told her I hoped my aunt didn't ask her mother about the project we were *supposed* to be working on but Callie only laughed. "They'll be so busy I doubt if they'll even think about it. I was afraid they'd ask where I was going with my bow. That's an awfully big thing to hide, but I don't think they even noticed when I left. Could've been carrying a *cow* for all they knew!"

Callie laughed, and so did I but my laugh was kinda shaky and my legs felt like they were made of yarn. Callie told me where to stand so that she could keep me in sight and I could see if anyone was approaching, then took her position to shoot from the far end of the field.

Callie paused briefly to caress the cherished emblems around her neck, and I watched as she stood, positioned her arrow, and drew back the bow string.

Ziiiiing! Whack! The arrow whizzed across the empty field and penetrated the stack. It was still so dark I couldn't tell how far in it went but from where she stood, Callie didn't seem too pleased. Shaking her head, she was reaching for a second arrow from her quiver when I turned at the loud dry-leaf rustle of someone approaching from the woods behind us.

Noticing my alarm, Callie lowered her bow and stood frozen in place. Had someone followed us here? It was too late to run. Too late to hide.

Suddenly a golden brown streak that was Tassel bounded from the trees behind us, dashed past me and greeted Callie with a joyful bark.

"Shhh!" Laughing, Callie knelt beside the dog and put her arms around him. "Do you think you can keep him quiet for a minute?" she asked, turning to me. "I want to try one more shot. I know I can do better."

And so while I gave Tassel the very best tummy-rub I could give, Callie sent a second arrow into the far away stack.

"Hurry! Hurry!" I urged as with Tassel beside her she ran to retrieve her arrows. It was getting lighter by the minute and if she wasn't pleased with this shot we were running out of time. The sooner we left this place the better I would feel as I had a feeling someone had been watching us the whole time.

Although we were still surrounded by a thick gray mist, I could see her wide smile as she ran toward me, arrows in hand. "Four stalks! The first one only pierced three. Nell, that's the best I've ever done!"

"I'm proud of you," I said, and meant it. "Are you

going to tell Joseph?"

Both of us were out of breath as we hurried from the field and Callie didn't answer until we had almost reached the village. "I don't know," she told me. "I'll have to wait and see."

Chapter Eleven

I needn't have worried that my friend would be found out for what she did. The whole village was like a stew pot on the boil with all the activity that day. The smell from the cooking fires filled the air as people hurried about stirring pots, turning spits of meat, and adding wood to the blaze. With all the visitors about I found myself surrounded by people I didn't know but other than a curious glance or two, they paid me little mind.

Callie and I helped Miss Harriett and several other women who were keeping an eye on the younger children. Baby Helen was beginning to recognize me now and it made me feel special when she was put in my care.

When it was time for the stalk shooting to begin Callie and I left the smaller children in the care of some of the older women as she didn't want to miss the competition.

Callie had explained to me that the games were matched weeks before and because her father was the matcher, his people were responsible for furnishing the food. The matcher chose a person from each team who would decide who would shoot, and that person was called a witcher. Because the witcher called on only the strongest and most experienced shooters, Callie suspected her brother was afraid he wouldn't be allowed to take part. Not that he would admit it, of course. I watched as Joseph waited with the other members of his team, but if he was relieved when called upon to shoot, his expression remained the same.

Each shooter was allowed two arrows to begin with, and the number of stalks penetrated was recorded. When everyone had shot, they took aim from the other side of the field and shot again. Each stalk counted as a point, and when a competitor reached fifty points, he was named the winner.

The contest seemed to go on forever and it was almost dark by the time it was over and some of the shooters began to leave. Others huddled around the cooking fires for a late meal before bedding down at New Echota. A shooter from Oothcaloga reached fifty points first but the team Joseph was on had the most points by the end of the day.

"How did your brother do?" I asked Callie as we walked home together later.

She shook her head. "He's not talking but I heard one of the men on his team say something to him about it." Callie smiled. "Seems one of his arrows pierced three stalks."

"*Three?*"

"Shh! He doesn't know I know."

"Aren't you going to tell him?" I asked. But Callie didn't answer.

A few days later we had our first snow. When I awoke that morning a light frosting covered the ground and it continued to come down until Miss Sawyer dismissed us early for the day.

Outside, I took a deep breath and felt the sharp cold all the way down my throat. Even the air tasted of snow. Dodging snowballs, Callie, Kate and I took refuge behind Callie's family's smokehouse. "Why don't we build a snowman?" I suggested when the coast was clear, and so after a lot of discussion, we decided to make a snow lady.

"Why can't we make her a snow princess?" Kate asked. "We can make her a crown of cedar and decorate it with holly berries."

"And we can name her 'Snow White!'" I said, and then, of course, I had to tell them the story. "I brought my book of Grimm's Fairy Tales from home," I added. "You can read them if you like."

It took a long time to get Snow White to stick together but I thought she looked good when we finished although her nose kept falling off. Kate got cold and went home but I stayed to help Callie give our princess a necklace of pumpkin seeds left from the gourd soup her family had eaten the day before.

"Do you have snow where you live?" Callie wanted to know, and I told her about the heavy snow we'd had in March the year before. "It was deep enough for my brother Tom and me to slide down the hill behind the college in one of cook's big dish pans," I told her. "I tried to give our dog Gulliver a ride but it must have frightened him because he jumped out."

That had been one of the last times Tom had taken time to play with me, and I must have looked sad because Callie asked what was wrong.

"I was just thinking of my brother," I said. "I guess I must miss him." I didn't mean to cry but I suppose I did as I felt tears cold on my face and the heavy, heavy longing for home came over me. I wanted to see Papa and Lucy and Tom. I wanted to sleep in my own bed and wake in the morning to find Gulliver at my feet— although I wasn't supposed to let him in my bed.

Callie put a gloved hand on my shoulder. "You can have mine," she said, holding back a laugh.

And then of course I had to laugh too. "Have you told him yet?" I asked.

She shook her head. "I thought about it but decided not to. Besides, I'm almost sure he already knows."

"How can you tell?"

"Just by the way he acts. He seems a lot nicer. Of course he'll never admit it, but I think somebody was watching me shoot that day."

"And you believe it was Joseph?"

Callie's mother called for her to come in and help with her little sister and I knew Aunt Nancy would probably need some help as well.

Callie pounded her hands together for warmth as we said goodbye.

"Who else would care?" she called after me as I started home.

Chapter Twelve

Something was missing. It was way past the middle of December and not one mention of Christmas. Did they not observe Christmas here, I wondered. Yet we held church services every Sunday in the Council House. Even though Mr. Worcester, the regular minister, remained in prison because of his refusal to be licensed by the state, Methodist circuit riders sometimes filled in, staying with a family for the night, and often we heard sermons from one of the Moravian missionaries in the area.

And poor Papa. Would he still have friends and neighbors in for syllabub on Christmas Day as he always did? When darkness came, my brother Tom and his friends liked to explode India crackers causing Gulliver to hide under the bed and Lucy to throw up her hands and holler. The big kitchen behind our house would be bustling as our cook Patsy overlooked her helpers in the baking of mincemeat pies, gingerbread, and Washington cake with currants and spices. The Christmas cookies would have been made weeks before and stored in an earthen pot in the cellar to soften. With the assistance of Miss Mary Rose, I heaped the mantels with glossy magnolia leaves and fragrant cedar and pine, and on Christmas Eve the ladies of our tiny Methodist Church sometimes let me help decorate the altar with the same.

Who would be doing these things now?

Maybe I should ask Aunt Nancy or her friend Mrs. Boudinot but it seemed a selfish question now with everyone worrying about the state taking away their land.

"The United States government needs to hurry and take action to support our cause," I overheard my aunt say to Mrs. Worchester as they shopped in Mr. McCoy's store one afternoon. I knew others were getting impatient as well, tiring of the government dragging its feet.

Mrs. Worcester nodded as she fingered the fabric in a bolt of cloth. She still looked sad and frail after her recent illness and the death of their baby. "Your brother was right when he wrote in the paper of Georgia's disregard of Cherokee rights," she said. "It needed to be said. I just hope it will get some results."

Aunt Nancy considered a blue flowered cream pitcher, then, thinking better of it, put it back on the shelf. She looked as though she wanted to say something further, but only sighed and moved on to decide on a precious bag of wheat flour instead.

I held baby Helen while she selected a few other purchases before starting for home. Although the snow had long since melted, an icy wind whipped about us as we left the store as if it meant to lift us off our feet. Aunt Nancy quickly tucked a blanket around Helen and held her snugly against her, and I tugged down the hood of my cape leaving just enough space to see. Neither of us spoke in our eagerness to reach home as quickly as possible, but my aunt remained quiet as she set about preparing supper that evening and I asked if she felt well.

Corncakes spattered on the hearth as Aunt Nancy spooned batter into the pan. Wiping her hands on her apron, she stood and smiled at me. "I suppose I'm just tired," she told me. "Tired of waiting for something to happen. It seems we've been waiting forever."

"Mrs. Worcester seems to think that what Mr. Boudinot writes in *The Phoenix* will encourage the people in Washington to help," I said, hoping it might make her feel better.

My aunt shook her head. "And only a few weeks ago, Buck wrote an editorial defending the progress of civilization," she said, referring to her brother by his childhood name. "Now I'm in favor of progress, too, but the State of Georgia doesn't seem to be aware of it."

No more was said about the subject that day as I think my aunt was trying to keep up her spirits when Uncle John came home from the print shop weary and smudged with oily black ink which no amount of scrubbing would wash away.

After supper I cleared away the dishes while my aunt nursed Helen. Uncle John, quiet during the meal, settled by the fire before speaking his mind.

"We seem to be mired in a gully," he said. "Can't go forward, and don't want to go back. Keep waiting for news from Washington—something to hope for—and I know it's the same for Elias. I can't image how discouraged he must be." Sighing, he lit his pipe, puffing until a red ember glowed.

Aunt Nancy managed a smile. "Still, you both manage to keep the paper in print."

"Yes . . . well . . . death announcements, marriages, and of course baptisms now and then . . ."

"Don't forget those accounts of thievery and drunkenness," my aunt offered.

Smiling, Uncle John held out his arms for the sleeping baby. "But wouldn't it be good to print something positive for a change?"

What about Christmas? That's positive. But not one word about the upcoming holiday, and it occurred to me I didn't even know what day it was. Why, Christmas might even be tomorrow—or worse still, yesterday!

"Do you know what day it is?" I asked my uncle when Aunt Nancy stepped away to heat water over the fire.

He shifted the sleeping baby to his shoulder. "Why, I believe it's Wednesday, Nell."

"But what day of the month?"

"Oh. It's the twenty-first. December twenty-first." Yawning, my uncle gently laid his sleeping daughter in her cradle.

In four days it would be Christmas and no one had even mentioned it.

Would it be all right with God if I reminded Him in my prayers?

Later, kneeling on the cold floor beside my bed I did just that.

The classroom was quiet except for a charred log crumbling in the fireplace. With a look from Miss Sawyer one of the older boys left his seat to replace it as the rest of us sat reading a story, "The Boy Who Stole Apples," from the *Blue Back Speller*.

I glanced at Callie and could tell that she, like me and some of the others, had finished reading the story right away. Soon we would review it with struggling younger readers, helping them with the more difficult words. It seemed a long time since I had my breakfast of milk and oatmeal and I eyed longingly the lunch pails lining the windowsill.

"Meet you by the tree," Callie mouthed silently as we were finally dismissed for lunch, and I scooped up my pail and filed out with the others. It was too cold to sit on the ground so some of us had made crude benches using logs held up by stones and it had become a favorite gathering place.

The question had worried me all day. I wanted to ask, but what if I didn't like the answer? Maybe they didn't observe Christmas here.

Suddenly, I wasn't so hungry anymore.

"Aren't you going to eat that cheese?" Kate asked, eyeing mine.

I broke off a piece and gave it to her, keeping some for myself as I knew it would be a long time until supper.

Callie frowned. "What's wrong, Nell? Aren't you hungry?"

Well, I *had* to know. "Don't you have Christmas here?" I finally asked.

Callie examined her apple. "What do you mean?"

"Well, no one's even *mentioned* it. Sunday will be Christmas Day and I haven't heard a word. By this time next week it will *all be over*!" I think I must have raised my voice at least an octave, and embarrassed, I gulped back tears.

"Silly! Christmas is going to happen whether anyone mentions it or not." Nudging me with her elbow, Callie laughed.

Kate's friend Susanna edged closer. "But last year we sang carols—remember?" She looked at the others. "On the last day of school before Christmas Miss Sawyer let us sing carols around the piano."

"And everyone got a trinket," Kate added. "Mine was a tiny storybook no bigger than . . . than . . . my baby sister's hand. I still have it."

"It won't be the same without Mr. Worcester here." Callie spoke softly. "Still, I heard Mrs. Worcester and Mrs. Boudinot plan to decorate the Council House with evergreens for the Christmas service. Maybe they'll let us help," she added, turning to me.

Our teacher blew the horn summoning us back inside and I hurried to cram what was left of my lunch back into my pail. "Maybe they will," I said, getting in line with the others.

And for the first time that day I found myself smiling.

Chapter Thirteen

"Why, I'm sure Mrs. Boudinot would be glad to have you and Callie help decorate for the service Sunday," my aunt said when I questioned her after school. "I only wish our dear Mr. Worcester could be here to conduct it." And then she smiled. "Well, at least you shouldn't have trouble finding plenty of cedar and pine."

"Will your brother . . . will Mr. Boudinot be here for Christmas?" I asked, thinking of their three small children.

"Oh, I wish it were so. As you've probably heard, the state has made it difficult to cover expenses for our printing supplies and Buck is in Philadelphia trying to find help with funds to keep it in print."

I knew that Mr. Boudinot and Mr. Worcester, with the help of my uncle John, had printed a Cherokee edition of the Gospel of St. Matthew and a hymnal in that language in addition to their work on the newspaper. And in one edition of *The Phoenix* I had even read articles about the beneficial effects of laughter, the excavation of Pompeii, and the evils of alcohol in addition to the local news.

"Mrs. Worcester looks tired to me," I said. "She must wish her husband would just go on and take that oath to support the laws of the state so he could come back here and be with his family. I would if he were my husband."

My aunt folded the garment she was sewing for Helen and set it aside. It was a deep twilight blue with tiny pink flowers we had admired earlier in Elijah Hicks' store.

"It's true Ann Worcester isn't as lively as she was before their baby's death and her own illness, but she's stronger than you think. Things aren't always as simple as they seem," she told me. "Although I'm sure she would like nothing better, it would go against something her husband firmly believes in, as does she."

Having become discouraged with my earlier attempts at sewing, I had sent by post weeks before two of my watercolor paintings as gifts for Papa and Lucy. For Papa I had painted a picture of Tassel sleeping on the Council House steps; Lucy's was a painting of the old hickory tree by the village spring just as its golden leaves were beginning to fall. My brother would receive a copy of the Twenty-third Psalm printed by our uncle in English and Cherokee. I hoped they would arrive in time for Christmas.

The three small Boudinot children were fair like their mother, and Eleanor, the oldest, was among the younger children in Miss Sawyer's school. Although her stubby legs made it hard for her keep up, she had pleaded so to go along to gather greenery that her mother didn't have the heart to deny her.

"Don't worry," I promised. "Callie and I can carry her if she gets tired."

Tiny Mrs. Worcester tied an apron around her middle and agreed to accompany us as well. Like Harriet Boudinot she spoke in an accent unfamiliar to me but her kind smile warmed me to her right away.

At her suggestion we headed down the familiar trail to the now-empty Worcester home where we were told we would find a large holly tree. With Eleanor bolting ahead, we took our time, pausing along the way to collect a few pine boughs and fragrant branches of cedar. Our voices seemed lost in the cold, still air, and other than our crackling footsteps, the scurrying of a squirrel and the faint lowing of cattle in a distant pasture were the only sounds we heard. My breath came in puffs and I was glad of my warm boots and snug woolen cape, but isn't it *supposed* to be cold at Christmas? I remembered the welcoming warmth of a neighbor's fire and hot spiced tea while caroling with friends from our church the year before.

But I wasn't going to think of that.

And I wasn't going to think of the scary medicine woman whose house lay hidden far back in the trees as we neared the bridge over a narrow stream, and the overbearing fear I had experienced the night I went to her for help. Yet, I reminded myself, she had saved our little Helen with her strange skills, and if called upon I would do it all over again.

But I hoped I'd never have to.

Farther down the road on a slight hill we came upon the empty Worcester house where Mrs. Worcester led us to the large holly tree behind it and helped us to break off branches. She had brought along a basket that was soon filled with the prickly green foliage and red berries.

It made me sad to look at the large white house that had been home to her family before her husband was sent to prison and I wondered if she felt the same. Of course she did! How could she not? But Ann Worcester went about doing what she had come for, pausing only to tug little Eleanor's cloak more snugly about her before we started back.

As promised, Callie and I took time about being "horsey" with Eleanor on our backs and I was glad when we finally reached the village. Twilight had not yet fallen but the faint light of candles shone from a few of the windows and the woodsy smell of smoke trailed from chimneys.

Harriet Boudinot greeted us on our return, and leaving Eleanor with some of her older cousins, joined us to help place evergreens in the Council House. The Boudinot home, I noticed, seemed to always be filled with noise and people as many of his nieces and nephews stayed there a lot. Even though it was a large house, I wondered where she put them all, but she didn't seem to mind. We had filled our aprons as well as Ann Worcester's large basket and soon had sprigs of holly and pine on the table that served as an altar. Fronds of spicy cedar and pine cones filled some of the wide windowsills, and tomorrow candles would be lit for the service. I closed my eyes, took a deep breath, and sighed.

"What are you doing?" Callie wanted to know.

I smiled and took another breath. "Inhaling Christmas," I told her.

It was not quite dark when I reached home and the spicy smell of gourd soup simmering over the fire reminded me I was hungry.

"How would you like to sing carols at the Boudinots?" Aunt Nancy asked in greeting, and I was so surprised all I could do was nod and smile.

"I thought we'd have an early supper tonight and

our Christmas meal tomorrow. And I hope to have a surprise for you after the service," she told me.

"What kind of surprise?" I looked about. The table was set with bowls and spoons for the soup with a crusty loaf of bread still warm from the fire but that was all. "Is it something to eat?"

My aunt laughed. "You'll see." She exchanged a look with Uncle John like they shared some kind of secret, but I could see he didn't plan to tell me either.

With my aunt's help I arranged the Christmas greenery on the mantel and even had some left for the table Aunt Nancy had spread with a white cloth, and we ate our supper by the soft glow of candles.

I could hear someone playing the piano as the three of us started across the way to our neighbors. The moon lit our path but my uncle carried a lantern in case we needed the light on our return.

Christmas Eve. What were Papa and Tom doing tonight? Would carolers come and sing for them? Would Patsy make our favorite dessert? I had received another letter from Papa a few days before telling me they all missed me and that he was getting stronger and Dr. Means seemed pleased with his recovery. I even had a short letter from my brother in which he said he was studying hard at the College and wished I could be with them for Christmas. Neither of them had mentioned the possible arrival of a new governess. It seemed I was here to stay—for a while at least.

The clear sweet voice welcomed us as we passed

through the white picket gate leading up to the Boudinots' home where candles gleamed from the windows.

While shepherds watched their flocks by night, all seated on the ground,
The angel of the Lord came down, and glory shone around.

Taking my uncle by the hand, I hurried up the walkway. *Christmas was here in New Echota.*

I was surprised to find Miss Sawyer there as were several of my classmates, including Callie and her family. Mrs. Boudinot welcomed all of us around the piano and everyone joined in singing the carol, *Silent Night*, even those who weren't familiar with the words, and I soon learned my uncle's sweet tenor carried over all the rest.

It had been Harriet's clear soprano we had heard when approaching the house, and Aunt Nancy and Ann Worcester soon joined her in leading us in the familiar carols, *Joy to the World* and *Hark! The Herald Angels Sing.*

Later we were served ginger cakes while one of the Worcesters' older children taught the younger ones the circle game of Drop the Handkerchief. I noticed Ann Worcester laughing at some of their antics when she happened to glance at Harriet across the room. Suddenly she looked away. She wasn't smiling anymore; nor was Harriet.

Would there be another Christmas here in this place? And another after that? To live with not knowing day after day must surely be stealing joy from *their* world.

I could hardly sit still during the church service the next

day for thinking about Aunt Nancy's surprise. I knew she had stayed up late after we got home the night before and woke to the tempting smell of chicken stew keeping warm on the hearth. Was that the surprise? I asked, but my aunt only shook her head.

Christmas Day had dawned brisk and cold and as we walked to Council House a few tiny snow flakes fluttered to the ground. While inside it was hard to resist looking out the windows to see if it had accumulated. Kate, who sat with her family in front of us, was reprimanded by her mother several times for doing just that.

I usually like the hymn-singing part of the service, but today I thought we could've done with fewer, and Reverend Jesse Bushyhead, the Baptist circuit rider, preached so long an old fellow across from us fell asleep and began to snore.

There was no sign of snow as we filed outside, but my disappointment didn't last long as I would soon find out what surprise was in store for me. Of course I had to wait while my aunt and uncle paused to speak with the minister and friends who had gathered there.

I set the table with the familiar flowered china while my aunt nursed Helen and Uncle John built up the fire. I was so hungry from all the good smells I shoved my impatience aside as we sat down to a hearty stew of chicken and winter vegetables, smoked ham, stewed peaches, dried from last summer's crop, and pickles. Afterward, I was so full I didn't think I could take another bite. But that was before Aunt Nancy brought out the first of her surprises.

"Your papa tells me this was a favorite of yours," she said, removing the lid from an earthenware pot. "I hope you won't be disappointed."

"Birds nest pudding!" I sniffed. It smelled the way it should. It looked the way it should. I dipped a spoon into my bowl and made happy noises. It tasted just like Patsy's. The ingredients, of course, didn't include birds' nests. It was made of cored apples baked in a custard of milk, sugar, and cream.

"This was a favorite of your mother's and mine when we were growing up," my uncle told me as he ate the last of his serving, and I had had no trouble finding room for mine as well.

I cleared the table while Aunt Nancy heated water for dishwashing over the fire. She had tried especially hard to make this Christmas a happy one for me and I thanked her with a hug. Now was the time to bring out my painting of the print shop I had hidden earlier in my dresser. "This is for both of you," I said, hoping they would like it. And they did—at least it seemed so, and Uncle John promised to make a frame for it and hang it on the wall for everyone to see.

"Thank you for making this a special time for me," I said. "It's been a happy Christmas."

My aunt laughed. "And it's not over!" She reached under their bed to bring out a mysterious box and a package wrapped in brown paper.

"The package is from me," she told me. "The box from your father came by post a week or so ago."

I opened the package first to find a dress made of the same pretty flowered print she had been working on for days. It had a tucked bodice, full sleeves above the elbow, and tiny buttons down the front. I held it to my chin. "It's beautiful! But I thought you were making it for Helen."

"I'm afraid it will be a while before she grows into that," Aunt Nancy said. "Now, let's see what your papa sent."

"I'd rather you open it." For some reason my hands felt weak and kind of shaky.

Inside were gifts for everyone: a soft little bonnet for Helen, a black silk cravat for Uncle John, a dainty white fichu, which is a kind of fancy lace collar, for my aunt. And for me two heavy books: *The Sketchbook of Jeffery Crayon, Gent*, containing the stories of "The Headless Horseman" and "Rip Van Winkle" as well as others, by American writer Washington Irving.

I slept with them under my pillow.

Chapter Fourteen

It was one of those clear winter days that made you feel if you only had wings, you'd be able to fly. The sky was so crystal blue it looked like it might shatter, and it was warm enough in the sun that I soon shed my cloak. That morning one of the small Hicks children had become so ill and fretful an older sister had to take him home and Miss Sawyer had given us a little more time for our noon break. Maybe she needed it even more than we did, I thought, and Callie and I sat on the front steps of the Council House to eat our lunch. Or at least, I did. Callie nibbled a hard boiled egg and shoved her pail aside.

I frowned. "What's the matter? You aren't sick, are you?" Several classmates had been absent because of coughs and colds, but Callie shook her head and shifted her feet on the step below us. Two of the older boys tossed another boy's hat back and forth in a game of "keep away' until his older brother intervened. With a lot of laughter and shouting, Kate and her friends played a game of tag, scudding around the maple tree to avoid being caught.

Callie looked up at them and sighed. "Look how happy they are, Nell. What's going to happen to them—to us—a year from now? A month from now?"

"Uncle John says Reverend Worcester has applied

to the Supreme Court and expects a hearing sometime soon," I reminded her. "And Aunt Nancy's brother Elias and John Ridge have been in Philadelphia to get people to protest so the federal government will support us." It suddenly occurred to me that without thinking, I had said *us* when referring to the Cherokees, but Callie didn't seem to notice.

"Anyway, it seems to have done some good," I continued. "Six thousand people signed a petition to Congress supporting the Cherokee cause. *Six thousand!*"

"But will it really help?" She looked at me with sad dark eyes. "I heard my parents whispering last night. They were talking about leaving."

"Oh, Callie, no!" My lunch sat like a stone in my stomach. "Where would you go?"

"They were talking about the Arkansas Territory."

Arkansas? I tried to picture a map of the States in my mind. Arkansas was a different color because it wasn't a state, and it was three states away unless you traveled the length of Tennessee. "But you can't! You just can't. I'd never see you again."

She didn't have time to answer because just then Miss Sawyer came out and blew her horn to summon us inside. Callie was the best friend I'd ever had and now it seemed I might lose her. And not just her, I remembered. If the Cherokees were forced to remove my uncle and aunt would follow, and so would the Boudinots, the Worcesters, and all the people I had come to care about.

"Why the sad face?" my aunt asked when I returned from school that afternoon. She sat at her spinning wheel with the firelight on her face while Helen kicked and waved her tiny arms about on a pallet beside her and it made such a peaceful picture I wanted to march down to Milledgeville and shake somebody.

I told Aunt Nancy what Callie had said about leaving.

"It's too early to think of that now." She looked up briefly from her work.

"Elias and John Ridge are still in Boston and expect a decision soon." Her voice was bright, but I don't know if she really believed what she was saying or was just trying to put me at ease.

"But what if the Supreme Court decides against them? What will happen then?"

She only smiled. "I prefer to hope for the best rather than prepare for the worst."

I sat on the floor to play with Helen who smiled and blew bubbles at me. "And what if the worst happens anyway?"

"Well then, we'll deal with that if and when the time comes."

I tried to take my aunt's advice not to worry about the court's decision but to say a prayer instead. But I remembered how hard I had prayed that I wouldn't have to go and live in New Echota, and look what had happened anyway. Of course I didn't know at the time about the welcome I'd receive and the new friends I'd make here. But I guess God knew all along.

"You are coming, aren't you?" Callie asked at school a few days later. "Anyone who paints as well as you shouldn't have trouble sewing."

I laughed. "You haven't seen my attempts at embroidery." They were so awful even Lucy couldn't find anything good to say about them, and she liked almost everything I did—or pretended to anyway.

"But it will be fun, and there'll be cakes and good things to eat. Besides, the ladies there will help you. You know how patient and kind Mrs. Worcester is . . . you'll catch on in no time."

There was to be a quilting party at the Boudinots' on Saturday and I knew Aunt Nancy planned to be there as did Callie's mother and several other women. Once Lucy had let me piece squares together for a patchwork quilt she was making for my doll, and I tried, but I think she had to do most of it over.

Maybe I could just watch, I thought, or help by entertaining the smaller children.

But I should've known that wasn't going to happen.

"Oh, Nell, I'm so glad you've come to help," Harriet Boudinot said in greeting as my aunt and I arrived with Helen, who was immediately whisked away by one of the older girls to be cared for in another room.

"But I really don't know . . . I don't know how . . . I'm not very good at sewing," I stammered.

"Good, then you can join the others." With a hand on my shoulder, she guided me to a corner of the room where several others were gathered. "Mrs. Worcester is going to show you how it's done so you'll be able to take your place around the frame."

Ann Worcester smiled as I took a seat in the only empty chair. "Chintz Stars isn't a difficult pattern and we have some practice pieces already cut so you can learn how to stitch them to the backing."

I glanced at Callie who had the nerve to laugh, then tried to hide it. "I really don't think—" I began . . .

She patted my shoulder. "This is to be a parting gift for friends who plan to leave soon for the west, so it needs to be finished before then. Many hands make light work, you know."

What could I do? I accepted my practice square and gave what I hoped was a threatening look at Callie. But traitor that she was, she wouldn't meet my eyes and was already busily sewing at the quilting frame with others more accomplished.

After several tries, I finally managed to knot my thread and began to practice making stitches to hold the star to the backing. It seemed simple enough, but I soon discovered that anything that seems simple isn't. The needle has to go all the way through and then back up again in tiny stitches that didn't wander. Mine wandered.

My star was made up of eight calico diamonds: four in a red flowered design, and four in a blue stripe that had already been sewn together in a pattern, and after a number of clumsy attempts, Mrs. Worcester said I was making progress. Frankly, I don't think she seemed convinced.

Quilters sat around a makeshift frame made by propping two long pieces of wood and two shorter ones on the backs of four ladder back chairs. When the stitching was completed on each long side of the quilt, that side would be turned under until the quilters would finish in the middle.

"We're going to miss John and Mary Ann," Harriet said after taking her seat at the frame. "Isn't there some way you can convince them to stay longer?" she asked, addressing my aunt.

"Don't think we haven't tried." Aunt Nancy shook her head. I don't know what they'll do without him in the print shop, and, of course it saddens me to lose my sister."

I had learned earlier that my uncle's assistant, John Candy, and his wife intended to leave the area before they were forced to remove. Mary Ann was a sister to my aunt, as well as to Elias Boudinot.

"I do wish they'd give it more time." Ann Worcester spoke quietly. "After all, we haven't yet heard the Court's decision."

I didn't look at Callie's mother but I wondered if she might reconsider leaving after listening to the conversation.

"Where do they plan to go?" someone asked my aunt.

She hesitated before answering. "Tennessee first, I suppose, then perhaps Arkansas or Oklahoma. If Mexico's president hadn't banned immigration from the States, they might've even considered going as far as Texas."

"Let's hope it won't come to that. It's just not right." Mrs. Worcester looked down at my mangled square. "Those of you who believe you're ready can move on the quilting frame and give others a break if you like."

Well, I didn't like and I wasn't ready so I was relieved when some of the older girls came in with a tray of cakes and tea.

I was enjoying a second ginger cake when we heard the rumble of horses approaching and frantic footsteps crossed the porch before someone pounded on the door.

Chapter Fifteen

Were we being attacked? Was the house on fire? I was so startled by the shouting and uproar, what was left of my ginger cake ended up as a handful of crumbs in my fist, and one of the young Worcester girls sitting next to me grabbed my arm in a grip so tight I had to pry her hand away.

Harriet Boudinot rose from her chair and was on her way to the door when Aunt Nancy stopped her. "Don't go, Harriet! You don't know who's out there." And she hurried from the room, probably to see to Helen and the other children.

The rest of us crowded around Mrs. Boudinot as if to band together to defend ourselves if necessary.

Thank goodness it wasn't necessary. "Wait a minute!" Mrs. Boudinot held up a hand for quiet. Someone was calling her name.

"Mrs. Boudinot! Mrs. Boudinot! Great news! We have glorious news! The Supreme Court has ruled in our favor!"

Harriet Boudinot, recognizing a friend's voice, rushed to fling open the door where the messenger was immediately surrounded and flooded with questions.

Ann Worcester's small face flushed with excitement. "This means my husband and Dr. Butler will be released from prison! They'll soon be home."

"Has anyone notified my brother at *The Phoenix?*" My aunt glanced at the print shop across the way where her brother, Stand Watie, was acting as editor during Elias Boudinot's absence.

She was assured that they had been told of the news, and then, of course, everyone wanted to know how it had all come about. We were told the United States Supreme Court had ruled as unconstitutional the law which had imprisoned the missionaries as well as the whole Indian code the state had established.

After the excitement settled, Mrs. Boudinot called everyone together to read the Court's decision aloud:

> *The Cherokee Nation then, is a distinct community, occupying its own territory, with boundaries accurately described, in which the laws of Georgia can have no force, and which the citizens of Georgia have no right to enter but with the assent of the Cherokees themselves or in conformity with treaties and the acts of Congress.*

Of course with all the whooping and hooraying, we all forgot about the quilt until Mrs. Worcester reminded us that as far as she knew, the Candys still planned to move, and I abandoned my attempts at needlework to help with the babies and small children, leaving others to work on their gift.

Everyone was too excited to eat at supper that night, although we must have eaten something as friends and relatives were constantly in and out of the cottage and there was no shortage of food on the table. A pot of corn meal mush sweetened with honey simmered on the hearth, and others brought bread, cheese, cider, and crocks of applesauce.

My aunt's brother, Stand Watie, spoke to those assembled saying that finally they could overcome the trials and sorrows of the last three years and claim their national sovereignty. And Harriet Boudinot, sitting by the fire with little William, the youngest of her three, reminded us that earlier, her husband had written that the question is forever settled as to who is right and who is wrong.

To the people in that small room that night there was no doubt.

Although it was February and frost lay on the ground, there was a feeling of spring when we gathered in the Council House for school the following Monday. I felt as if all the stale gray winter air had been sucked out and replaced by something fresh and light. The others must have felt it too; even Miss Sawyer greeted us with a smile to begin the day.

"I'm sure you've all heard by now that Justice John Marshall has announced that only the United States government can legislate for Indians, and Georgia laws are null and void where we're concerned," she told us. "Our dear Mr. Worcester and Dr. Butler will soon be coming home."

And the whole class stood and cheered.

"I wonder how long it will take," I said to my aunt a few days later.

She stopped to wipe Helen's face. She'd been feeding her oatmeal and it looked to me like she had more on the outside of her than the inside. "How long will what take?" she asked.

"For the missionaries to come home. Mrs. Worcester must be excited. I guess she'll be ready to move back into her own place now."

Aunt Nancy frowned. "It should've been immediate, so I expect he'll be here in a few days. And I know Buck's eager to get back to the paper, too. John seems to think he'll be home before too long as well."

To celebrate I set the table with the good china on Aunt Nancy's lace-trimmed cloth. A pot of cabbage soup made with smoked ham kept warm on the hearth, and the soft light of candles cast shadows in the dark corners of the room. It seemed everything would turn out all right after all.

But then it didn't.

It wasn't unusual for my uncle to come home well after dark, especially if he was working on an issue of *The Phoenix* or some other important printing job, but tonight the hours seemed to drag. Helen had been fed, rocked, and tucked in her little bed and my aunt let the fire burn down low while our supper kept warm on the hearth.

At the sound of Uncle John's tread on the doorstep, Aunt Nancy hurried to dish up the soup, but after one look at his bleak expression she set the ladle aside.

"John, are you ill?" She hurried to his side. "What's wrong? Tell me!"

Without a word he sank into the nearest chair and covered his face with his hands.

Stooping beside him, she took his hands in hers. "What is it, John? What happened? Is it Buck? You have to tell me." Her voice, usually as calming as a lullaby, seemed as if it might crumble into pieces.

My usually jolly uncle, who loved making Helen laugh, and only two short months before had burst out with "Joy to the World" as if he meant for heaven and earth to hear, looked well-deep in misery.

"It seems the State of Georgia has decided to ignore the Supreme Court's ruling, and President Jackson is refusing to enforce it," he said.

My aunt stood suddenly. "Can he do that?"

"It seems so." Uncle John shook his head. "Who has the power to stop him?"

"We have to try!" Aunt Nancy sighed. "It seems President Jackson has a short memory."

When I asked what she meant, my uncle explained that a large body of Cherokees had volunteered to help the army led by then General Jackson in the Battle of Horse Shoe Bend. "In the war between the United States and the Creeks back in 1814," he said, "a brave Cherokee named Charles Reese was responsible for the Cherokees attacking from the rear. It weakened the Creeks' front, resulting in their ultimate defeat."

"This all seemed to start with the discovery of gold in the eastern part of the Nation," Aunt Nancy said. "Greed! Pure greed."

I wanted to comfort them, but what could I do? It was so unfair, and they seemed helpless to change things.

"How can the state ignore the Supreme Court?" I asked. "Don't they have more power than Georgia law?"

My uncle explained to me that a few years ago the state legislature had passed an edict to cancel Cherokee authority and assert Georgia sovereignty over the territory.

"That's why they aren't allowed to take care of tribal affairs in their own Court House or Council House," he said, "but are forced to conduct such matters in Alabama or Tennessee."

My aunt led him to the table. "Come. Sit down and have something to eat, John. Maybe things will seem clearer in the morning, but it does seem to be getting harder and harder to find someone who will take our side. Just last summer Chief Justice Marshall ruled we couldn't hold the status of a foreign nation, and now we aren't even allowed to be a separate state."

Uncle John looked up at her over his bowl of soup and managed a smile. "Don't forget the words on the mast of *The Phoenix*," he reminded her. "I will arise."

It was summer and I was in the garden back home in Athens making a daisy necklace for Gulliver, only he wouldn't be still for me to put it around his neck. Patsy sat on the back porch stringing beans. They thudded as they hit the bottom of the big pan she held in her lap. Bees buzzed around the tangle of roses on the trellis filling the air with their sweet pink smell.

Gulliver suddenly bounded away at the sound of horse's hooves thudding around the house and my father pulled up on Liberty and jumped from the saddle.

Papa! Your leg has healed! I shouted and jumped up to greet him, but he pounded up the steps, urging me into the house before him. "We have to leave . . . we have to get out! Hurry and get your clothes together—now!"

"But where? Why?"

"Don't argue, Nell! Just do as I say. This place isn't ours anymore. We must go!"

"Not ours? But it's home. It's *our* home!" I looked around for Lucy. Lucy would make everything right.

"Lucy! Lucy!" But Lucy wasn't there.

"Nell, Nell! Wake up. You're having a nightmare."

Aunt Nancy stood over my bed, her cool hand on my forehead. "Shh! You're here now. Go back to sleep. It's all right."

But I knew it wasn't.

Chapter Sixteen

Most of my classmates had already learned of the disappointing news when I arrived at school the next day. I felt especially sorry for the Worcester children who must surely be discouraged that their father would not be returning soon, and little Eleanor Boudinot was not her usual lively self. From what I'd overheard my uncle say, it seemed likely that Elias Boudinot would not come home until he had done everything in his power to try and make things right.

Miss Sawyer did her best to conduct classes as always and I could see she was making an effort to stay calm, although I thought her words seemed forced and stiff.

"I know many of you are saddened, as I am, at this recent distressing news, but we mustn't give up hope. This isn't over yet; remember, we have justice on our side," she told us.

I wanted to cover my face and hide when Callie's brother Joseph spoke up. "The white people already have all the land they can use. Why do they want ours?" he asked.

Our teacher didn't answer right away but leaned on her desk and sighed. Being white, too, I wondered if she felt as ashamed as I did. Then, standing taller, she spoke in a firmer voice. "My advice to all of you is to get all the education you can when you can. If, by chance you *are* removed to a place where you can't attend school, then you'll be prepared to teach others."

"I'm sorry about what Joseph said," Callie told me during noon break. "Sometimes he just doesn't think before he speaks. I'm sure he didn't mean to hurt you."

I was sure he did, but I didn't want to talk about it. It would just make me feel worse. "Are your parents still planning to leave?" I asked, although I wasn't sure I wanted to hear her answer.

"They haven't said any more about it. I think they're waiting to hear what's going to happen now. I guess we all are."

March was a little over a week away and even though it was still cold and damp, most of our classmates seemed glad of the brief freedom to be outside with the sky for a ceiling—even if it was gray and cloudy. Aunt Nancy said lambing season would be here before long, and as soon as it was dry enough, fields would be plowed and planted for the summer crops. It couldn't happen soon enough for me. New life. New growth. New hope.

John Candy and his family had left, Miss Sawyer had told us, and we would soon be holding classes in their empty house since it was smaller and easier to keep warm.

"I guess Miss Sawyer will need our help moving things to the Candy house," Callie said as we walked back inside at the sound of the horn.

She nudged me and frowned. "Why are you laughing?"

"It sounds like a fairytale," I explained. "Like in *Hansel and Gretel*. We'll be going to school in a candy house. Hope we won't find a witch in there."

Callie ducked her head and whispered, "Well, there are some who think Miss Sawyer is, but I think she's nice, at least most of the time I guess."

And I thought she was too.

Early in March the weather turned fair, and the middle of the first week, Miss Sawyer decided, would be a good time to move. The morning had started out cold with a thin crust of frost on the ground, but by the noon hour we were able to eat our lunch in comfort on the sun-warm steps of the Council House.

Much to our delight she dispensed with our lessons for the rest of the afternoon in order to form a procession to move the things we would need in our new classroom. Two of the older girls had gone ahead to sweep out the house and clear it of dust and cobwebs as the Candys had been gone for several weeks. One of the boys had ridden his mule to school that day and was able to carry much of the heavier things in one trip.

Callie and I led the younger children in *Here We Go 'Round the Mulberry Bush* and we made a game of our short trip across the green to our small schoolhouse. We had not learned anything further from President Jackson about his intention not to uphold the decision of the Supreme Court of the country, and the whole of the tiny community had been under a gray spell. But most, I noticed, seemed to relish the small things in an attempt, I suppose to snatch what pleasure they could while they could.

Callie and I were helping some of the others stack books on a shelf in the front of the room when we heard a shrill scream and rushed to the door to find Little Will doubled up on the ground holding his leg. I could see blood staining his trousers above the knee.

"The mule kicked him," Joseph explained, kneeling by his side. "He was helping us unload and I guess he got too close."

I had never seen Little Will cry, but he was crying now and I wanted to shove everyone else aside in my rush to comfort him. I had been helping the little boy with his reading since my arrival at the school and found him to be quick to learn. I was as proud of him as if he had been my own brother and it hurt me to see him in pain.

"Here now, let me get this child inside!" With a flurry of skirts, Miss Sawyer shooed us aside and scooped the little boy in her arms. "Jack," she called over her shoulder to one of the older boys, "go and get Inola. Tell her what happened—hurry!"

I was glad I wasn't asked to go and fetch the scary medicine woman, but I would have, of course, to help Little Will. We followed our teacher inside where she laid the child on a table and began to carefully peel the bloodied pants leg away from the wound. Little Will cried even louder as she took water from the drinking pail and tried to clean the blood away.

"I'll try not to hurt, child, but I have to wash away the blood so I can see how badly you're hurt." Our teacher's voice was as soothing as I'd ever heard it and I could tell she hurt as much for Little Will as I did.

Miss Sawyer looked up at us gathered all around. "Callie, would you please give me a hand here?" she asked, and of course my friend hurried to oblige.

But Little Will struggled to sit up and cried out,

"Nell! Want Nell!" And he held out his little arms to me.

It was a good thing no one stood in my way because nothing was going to keep me from him. "I'm here, Will. I'm right here." Stepping aside, Callie nodded to me and I encircled his small body in my arms and assured him he was going to be all right. If Inola could make his pain go away, she couldn't get there soon enough.

Our teacher frowned as she examined the wound, and I forced myself to look as well. A mule is a large animal with a powerful kick and Will's small limbs were fragile. What if it had broken a bone? I looked up at Miss Sawyer with an unspoken question and she must have been thinking the same thing as she sighed and said, "Well, it appears no bones are broken, but this is a horrid gash. I'm afraid it's going to need stitches."

Of course Little Will howled at that and I didn't blame him. Dr. Butler was still imprisoned in Milledgeville. Who was going to stitch him up?

It turned out that Miss Sawyer had done this before and was prepared to do it again. Turning to one of our classmates she asked for her bag and for someone to go for Will's mother.

"I think she's down at the pen," someone called out. "Their cow, Adsila's calving."

"I'll find her," Kate said on her way out the door.

"Here! Take this bucket and stop by the well on your way back," Miss Sawyer called after her.

Little Will didn't seem to be as afraid of the medicine woman as he was of our teacher stitching him up, but he settled down some and let Inola apply a cold compress of mint leaves to soothe the jagged tear just above his knee.

I stepped aside to make room for Little Will's mother but she seemed to want me to stay and went to stand on his other side so that he could see her as well.

"If you'll be very brave, I'll sing to you," I whispered, and Little Will nodded and wiped his tears on the back of his hand. "Keep your eyes on the candle flame," I told him, "and think of good things, happy things, like playing in the sunshine and wading in the creek."

I focused on a knothole on the far side of the room so I wouldn't see what was taking place and began to sing. I made it through "Old King Cole," and "Little Bo Peep," and had begun "Mary Had a Little Lamb," when Little Will had enough of Mother Goose, and probably me as well, and let us know it in loud angry cries.

His mother made comforting noises and stroked his forehead but that didn't seem to help. I looked at our teacher for advice but she was busy with problems of her own and seemed to be depending on me to keep him still. Remembering a time when I was about Will's age and very sick with a fever, cough, and rash, Papa soothed me by telling me a story about a little girl with the very same name as mine. My interest was held even more by the fact that the Nell in Papa's story was only two inches high, could hide in a teacup, and could play all kinds of tricks without being seen.

"Guess what I saw in our garden last summer," I began. "A tiny little boy who was so small he drank out of a honeysuckle blossom, slept on a bed of dandelion fluff, and wore an acorn cap for a hat.

"And what do you think his name was? It was *Will* just like yours. Only he wasn't little Will, he was tiny, tiny Will because he wasn't any taller than . . . than . . . a teacup."

Little Will's understanding of English was much better than before but he still needed help from Callie to translate from time to time.

"He wants to know what kind of clothing he wore," Callie said.

"Why, his mother wove him beautiful clothes from the greenest grass," I told him, "and when that dried out, she just made him more. After all, there's plenty of grass and he always had something new.

"Tiny Tiny Will had a pet bird, a sparrow, and it would let him fly on its back wherever he wanted to go."

"He wants to know the bird's name," Callie said.

"Why, it was Sally . . . Sally Sparrow," I told him, glad I could think of something fast. "And one day Sally flew him way, way up high to the top of a mountain . . . and on top of that mountain was a castle.

"A king lived in that castle, and he was very tall and very fat. He was probably as tall as . . ." I looked about . . . "the top of this house. He would have to stoop to get in the door."

Little Will looked up at the ceiling. "What his name?"

"His name? His name was Gobble—King Gobble, because all he liked to do was eat. His favorite food was a soup that was made of everything good, and one day when the king fell asleep, Tiny Tiny Will had a taste of that soup. It was the best soup he had ever eaten and he wanted more, so every night after the king went to sleep he would help himself. He was so small and ate so little, the king probably wouldn't have noticed at all except one day he woke early and found poor Tiny Tiny Will eating his soup."

Poor Little Will looked so alarmed I quickly smoothed things over. "Well, Tiny Tiny Will thought this was going to be the end of him and started looking around for Sally. Maybe he could hop on her back and she could fly him out of danger before the king threw him in the dungeon—or whatever it is kings do to people who eat their soup.

"But instead the king plucked him up gently and placed him on the table. 'I lost my royal ring not long ago,' he said. 'It was a gift from my father and made of precious rubies and emeralds, but I can't reach it to get it back. It fell down a hole in the floor, you see—a very small hole. I know it's there, but there's no way I can reach it. If you will help me, not only will I let you go free, but I will also reward you.'

"So, of course Tiny Tiny Will was happy to help. It was easy for him to crawl into the hole and retrieve the king's ring," I said.

"He wants to know about his reward," Callie reminded me.

"Well, he wanted the recipe for the soup, of course, and he took it home to his mother so she could make it for him every night."

By that time Miss Sawyer had finished stitching the little boy's wound and the medicine woman applied a poultice made of the purple coneflower to keep down infection.

Little Will didn't say so, but I think he was disappointed with my character's reward at the end of the story, but at least it helped him over a rough spot.

And besides, I couldn't think of another ending.

Chapter Seventeen

Everything was going wrong. My aunt and uncle got up every morning; the baby was fed and changed, the fire replenished, food was prepared, Uncle John left for the print shop, and I set off for school as usual, but it seemed everyone was wandering on a road to nowhere. Only a few months before the village had celebrated a promised future with joy. Now, a big ugly spider had spun its sticky web over not only New Echota, but the whole Cherokee Nation, and there didn't seem to be any way out.

Still, babies took no notice of all this, nor did they care, and Little Helen had outgrown her tiny gowns. Wagons had just arrived from Augusta at Elijah Hicks' store and I held the baby while Aunt Nancy browsed over muslins, linens, and cards of lace and ribbons I cared absolutely nothing about. Shifting Helen onto my hip I found an upturned box in an out-of-the-way corner and sat down to wait.

"What news from your brother?" An older woman I knew only to be called Rebecca came to stand beside my aunt. She lifted a large empty basket to the counter and adjusted the shawl around her shoulders. "Is it true he's not standing firm? I can't think it so of Buck."

My aunt stiffened her shoulders and drew in her breath. "You must be aware that no one has worked harder for our cause than my brother. Have you not read his writings in *The Phoenix*? Surely you must know of his struggles to promote our progress and to keep the paper in print."

I was glad to see Elijah Hicks step up to the counter to bring their attention to a new display of decorative combs as I could tell Aunt Nancy was becoming upset.

"I well remember your brother's reply to a Mr. McKenney on the cost of the intended removal," he told her. "Buck suggested the United States government could put that money to better use by investing in schools and colleges throughout the Nation. It's a shame they didn't take his advice."

My aunt was silent as we walked home. Finally, I could keep quiet no longer. "What do you think will happen, Aunt Nancy? Can the President just ignore a ruling of the Supreme Court? It doesn't seem right."

She paused for a minute and shook her head. "No, Nell, it isn't right, yet our president is quoted as saying, 'John Marshall has made his decision; let him enforce it now if he can.'

"Years ago I remember reading a report by a group of missionaries near Chickamauga Creek. I'll never forget it. It said that the Indians didn't know how to understand their Father the President. He sent them a plough and hoe and said it wasn't good to hunt but they must cultivate the earth. Now he offers rifles for good hunting in Arkansas."

I remembered Miss Sawyer reading us a speech by John Ridge, one of the main leaders in resisting removal:

You asked us to throw off the hunter and warrior state: We did so—you asked us to form a republican government: We did so—adopting your own as a model. You asked us to cultivate the earth, and learn the mechanic arts: We did so. You asked us to learn to read: We did so. You asked us to cast away our idols, and worship your God: We did so.

Later that day I asked my uncle why the government wasn't satisfied after the Cherokees had tried so hard to please them. He leaned over to light his pipe with a twig from the fire and the tobacco came to life with a golden woodsy glow. "Well," he said after a puff or two, "I don't think they felt threatened as long as the Indians lived in a primitive way as they did for many years, but then things began to change. They owned land, farmed it, raised cattle, and, most of all, discovered the magic of the written word—not only through our alphabet, but their own syllabary. To put it briefly, they just don't want the competition. And they don't want to share the land. As our friend John Ridge said, 'It seems the President is saying now: I don't want to enforce it, and I won't.'"

Most Cherokees, I had learned, owned property, usually several acres, and some a lot more. Before I came to New Echota I didn't know Indians owned land; in fact I didn't know much about them at all. I thought most of them lived in the woods—probably in teepees, and it frightened me when I saw an Indian in town. I had never seen a teepee in New Echota, and the only person who frightened me was the medicine woman, Inola, and I was becoming more accustomed to her—at least during the daytime.

It's funny how things seem to happen together—sometimes bad things, sometimes good. This time it was good, but it was a long time coming. Aunt Nancy was teaching me to make butter and I was churning on the tiny front porch one sunny morning in early April when Mrs. Boudinot stopped by with a letter for me from Papa. I almost turned over the churn in my excitement to read it:

> *My Dear Daughter,*
> *With God's help, (and that of Dr. Means) I grow stronger every day and am now able to walk with a cane with little pain. I hope soon to be able to resume my teaching duties at the College when the next course of study begins.*
>
> *I have made several inquiries to find a qualified governess to replace Miss Mary Rose—or perhaps I should say, Mrs. Everett, and have received several encouraging replies. I hope you are making good progress in your studies there and are proving to be a help to your aunt and uncle.*
>
> *We miss you and pray that you remain well. Your brother sends his love, and Lucy is counting the days until you come home. With the help of Providence, that will be sometime in the coming summer.*
>
> *Your Loving Papa*

I could hardly wait to share my message and both Miss Harriett and Aunt Nancy rejoiced with me. Miss Harriett, too, had happy news to tell. Mr. Boudinot would soon be returning home.

But my aunt didn't seem as pleased about her news when I mentioned it to her later.

"Of course I'm glad for Harriett and her family, and

it will be good to see my brother again," she said, "but there are those who think he is giving up on the removal question, and that concerns me."

Our school at New Echota would not be holding classes again until the fall as even young hands were needed for the planting and growing season ahead. "Soon it will be time to plant the Three Sisters," Callie told me one day as we hunted wildflowers in her secret place.

"What are the Three Sisters?"

Callie stooped to point out a patch of the dainty white bloodroot flowers almost hidden in the underbrush. The sap, she explained, was used as a red dye.

"We learned about the Three Sisters from our Iroquois ancestors," she said, "and they're the three most important foods in our diet: corn, winter squash, and beans. We plant the corn first, then the beans to climb the cornstalks, and finally the squash is planted on the outside of the bed so the vines will have room to wander and also protect the other plants. They help each other, and that's why they're called the Three Sisters."

"If you're going to plant, then that must mean you plan to stay!"

"For a while at least," she said. "My father has hopes of the election of a new Great White Father to replace the one we have now."

"You mean President Jackson?"

She nodded, laughing. "I think some of the others are hoping for the same."

"Oh, Callie! Wouldn't that be grand?" I was being selfish, of course, because I didn't want her to leave, but it would also offer a bright thread of faith for all the

Cherokees, and other tribes as well.

Our baby Helen was beginning to crawl, which meant she wanted to get into everything, and if she couldn't put it in her mouth, she would reach for it with her quick little hands. Aunt Nancy stayed busy melting tallow for candles and pouring it into molds as we had used most of the family's supply during the winter months. I stayed busy keeping Helen away from the dangerous fire.

I finally got to meet Aunt Nancy's brother, *The Phoenix* editor, Elias Boudinot, when he stopped by one night. I listened to his voice as he spoke with my aunt and uncle late into the night, and his speech had a musical quality, so pleasing to the ear that I fought sleep. I didn't want to miss a word. When I woke the next morning I was disappointed to realize I had. Mr. Boudinot had been speaking of the importance of printing both sides of the removal question. From what I could understand, he agreed with John Ridge that the terms of the treaty should go before the Cherokee council so everyone would understand their choices, but Chief John Ross was determined to fight it. "It seems," he said, "we are being accused of treachery."

He was a handsome man: dark eyes, dark hair, and a warm smile, but an uneasy burden rested on his shoulders, and the pain of it was mirrored in his eyes.

Chapter Eighteen

"I think it's time for you to have a new bonnet," my aunt announced one bright April morning.

"But I already have a bonnet. Why do I need another?"

She laughed. "Do you need a reason for a pretty new bonnet? Your papa left money to buy these things, and I'm sure he expects you to use it."

"But there's nothing wrong with the one I have," I protested. I disliked wearing bonnets. They just got in the way and I was always tugging at the ribbons.

My aunt laid aside the dainty dress she was sewing for Helen and turned to me. "Don't you think that once in a while we just need something to brighten our day? And besides, we have a reason to wear something nice. We're going to a wedding."

"Really? Who's getting married? When?"

"My friend Rachel Adair is marrying next week, and I think everyone's ready to celebrate a happy occasion."

I remembered going to a cousin's wedding a few years ago. It took place in a large house outside of Eatonton and friends and relatives came from miles around and stayed for several days. The grownups were so busy with all the wedding festivities they kind of ignored the younger ones, and that suited us just fine. We had our fill of sweets and barbecue and played under the huge oak trees that surrounded the house until we were so tired we didn't even protest when bedtime came. Maybe a new bonnet wouldn't be such a bad idea after all, I thought.

"I guess it will be in the Court House," I said, since that was where church services were usually held. "Will the Reverend Bushyhead perform the ceremony?"

Aunt Nancy smiled. "Not this time, Nell. This will be a tribal ceremony. I can't remember the last time I attended one, and I'm glad you'll have an opportunity to see it."

She explained that the wedding ritual wouldn't be the religious kind we were accustomed to but a ceremony connected with the tribal union. I had no idea what that meant but looked forward to finding out, especially when I learned Callie, Kate, and others I knew from school would also be attending.

I chose a yellow straw bonnet with a wide brim trimmed in white frilly ribbons that tied with a bow in the back. I didn't expect to like it, but it surprised me when I looked at myself in the mirror in Mr. Hicks' store and a young lady looked back. Who was this strange person? Did I know her? Would I like her? I walked out of the store swinging the box with my new bonnet in it and feeling like I had turned into somebody else.

The day of the wedding turned out sunny and warm. Violets carpeted shady places now green with spring grass, and early roses tumbled around doorsteps. I wore my green striped dress with the leg of mutton sleeves and let the ribbons of my bonnet trail over my shoulder. Callie looked pretty in a new yellow dress with a big white collar; her bonnet was blue with yellow flowers around the brim, and Aunt Nancy sat up the night before adding a lacy ruffle to a green flowered dress I'd never seen her wear. It seemed everyone was trying to erase the disappointments behind them and look toward a brighter future. For a day at least.

I think nearly everyone in New Echota gathered in and around the Council House until I wondered if there would be room inside to hold them all. My uncle and aunt and I, with little Helen, were lucky to find seats downstairs and soon the second floor was full as well, with latecomers standing on the stairs. The room was blooming with color. The women wore their finest dresses, and although some of the men came in buckskin or calico, many wore a linen pullover shirt that was tucked into the pants, and a few came in more formal wear with a wrapped tie called a cravat that covered the neck. This was worn with a vest and sometimes a coat.

The room echoed with voices. Everyone seemed to be talking at once, mostly in Cherokee, although some spoke English. I looked for my friends and saw Callie and her family seated across the room. She waved at me then turned her attention to her little sister as Awinita was doing her best to climb over the back of the seat.

Suddenly the room grew quiet.

Jesse Wolf, the groom, Aunt Nancy had explained, had been feasted at a home not far from the Council House, and the bride and her female friends had been entertained in the same manner in a lodge on the opposite side.

I watched as the older men came in and took the highest seats on one side. Older women followed, taking seats on the opposite side. I was surprised when Uncle John and others rose and took a seat with the

older men. Aunt Nancy explained that the married men
sat together and the women would do the same. Then,
leaving Helen with me, my aunt went with the other
married women to join the older ones.

At some kind of signal, that I didn't hear or understand, the groom's friends escorted him to the open
space between the men and the women, and the bride's
companions did the same with her so that they stood
facing each other several feet apart.

A woman, whom I later learned was the groom's
mother, came out and gave him a blanket and a bulky-
looking parcel I was told was a smoked ham. The bride
then received from her mother an ear of corn and a
blanket.

What did this have to do with being married? I
wondered. It was nothing at all like the weddings we
had back home. I soon learned that Helen wasn't inter-
ested and didn't care one bit. She was teething and her
gums hurt. Long threads of drool oozed from her
mouth onto my shoulder and then down the front of
my dress. I rubbed her gums with my finger until she bit
me as hard as she could with her one tiny tooth, and it
was all I could do to keep from crying out.

I couldn't let her cries disturb the ceremony. I
would just have to take her outside. And then I discovered the paper-wrapped parcel Aunt Nancy had left in
my lap and the dried peach slices inside. Dried peaches,
I had learned, were good for feeding pigs, making pies,
and easing teething pain. I held the peach slice and let
Helen gum to her heart's content while pink slime made
a river down her new white dress and onto mine. But
she was happy—and quiet, at least for now, and I
watched as the bride and groom took slow steps to

finally meet in the middle. There the groom presented his ham and the bride her corn, and the blankets were united.

This meant, I was told, that he will provide meat for his family and she will furnish bread, and they will sleep in the same bed.

Afterward everyone went outside where we were treated to a lively display of dancing with a lot of drums and shouting and my friends and I ate our fill of roasted chicken, honey cake, and sweet strawberries until the fading sun splashed the sky in the west with flaming streaks of rose and gold.

Back home my brother wrote of his studies at the College of Virgil and Cicero and Roman antiquities, but I knew I was learning here more than he would ever be able to understand.

Chapter Nineteen

The month of April quickly passed into May. Fields of corn were planted and soon grew high enough to sow beans around the tender green stalks, and I was told pumpkins and winter squash would follow. From what I could understand, life in the village seemed to be faithful to its usual routine, yet a feeling of restlessness hovered, and even the gentlest people became irritable and jumpy. Their lives were not their own.

"It's like a big giant hand came down and just messed up our world," Callie said one day. "My father goes around like he has a rock tied around his neck and there's nothing I—or anyone can do about it."

I kept hoping President Jackson would change his mind, or our government would force him to go along with the court's decision, but nothing seemed to change. I wrote Papa to ask when he planned to run for the legislature as I knew he would do what he could to help, but was told the election wouldn't take place until fall. And maybe . . . just maybe . . . Jackson would be defeated.

"What do you think will happen, Uncle John?" I asked one evening as the two of us sat on the stoop: he with his pipe, and me, peeling potatoes for supper.

Shaking his head, he drew on his pipe before answering. "I wish I could predict that, Nell. I'm sure you know there are two factions on this issue, and each side thinks they're right. While in Washington, our friend John Ridge received a letter from an official on the American Board and it seems the political parties there believe we're fighting a losing battle and it would be useless to continue to defend our cause."

"Well . . . what do you think?" I asked.

He sighed. "I hate to admit it but some of the terms in the treaty they're offering sound tempting—if we can believe them. They say there's rich land west of the Arkansas territory, and many of the Cherokees have already relocated there. They're promising to subsidize them for the first year and pay them for the lands they leave behind, as well as to provide support for other things we'll need."

I frowned. "What kind of things?"

My uncle examined his pipe as if he could find the answer there. "Well Nell, they'll need schools, black-smiths—all the other essential structures, and materials to build them."

I tossed the last peeled potato into a bowl. "But what about the things they'd have to leave?"

Each family would receive blankets, axes, ploughs, and hoes, I was told, and every male adult would be given a rifle. They would also be provided with spinning wheels, looms, and other necessary household things, plus a guaranteed protection from hostile Indians in the area.

I didn't like the sound of that part about the hostile Indians. It seemed to me, I said, that things would just be whole lot easier if these people could just stay in the land they loved and take care of it as they'd been doing before our government came along and messed things up.

"Well, the thing is, Nell," my uncle told me, "the Cherokees will no longer be allowed to have their own government here. If they do decide to stay, they'll have to become citizens of the states where they live and lose the protection of the federal government."

I picked up my bowl to go inside. I wanted to express my displeasure, but couldn't find the words to do it.

"I know this upsets you, Nell," my uncle said. "It worries me too—more than I can say, and I feel it's tearing us all apart. I know John Ross, our principal chief, is decidedly opposed to it and he'll fight it to the end, but I think Mr. Boudinot and John Ridge have both wrestled with this demon and come to the conclusion that they have no other choice."

I didn't ask if he agreed with them. Just then I really didn't want to know.

Every time I passed Callie's home I was afraid to see it vacant as several families had already left for the west. I was sad to learn that Little Will and his people were among them, as were several members of the Wolf family. But corn was still growing in the field the Quinns tended and I hoped that meant they wouldn't leave at least until time for harvest.

"Well, it looks like things are going to liven up here in a week or so," Mrs. Worcester said to my aunt a few days later when we saw her at the spring. "I read in *The Phoenix* there's going to be a ball play with a team from Coosawattee, and I'm afraid there might be trouble."

"What kind of trouble?" I asked. I couldn't imagine why there would be a problem with playing with a ball.

Aunt Nancy frowned. "Usually when these teams

get together a lot of gambling, and of course, drinking takes place. Elias continues to advise against it in his writings, but it seems to do little good."

Mrs. Worcester scooped up a gourd full of the clear water for Ann Eliza. "We do need something to distract us from worrying about the threat looming over us. Let's just pray the good Lord will calm our hearts."

I glanced at my aunt and could tell by the look on her face that she thought the players might give the good Lord a little help of their own, but of course she didn't say so.

The game would be played, I learned, on a level field near the river and was to begin with dancing and chanting the night before. During my short time in New Echota I had witnessed chanting and dancing, but never like what I was to see the next week.

The night before the game, people walked or came on horseback from miles away to gather in a field, lured by the somber beat of the music and the women's soft voices as they sang the familiar ball songs.

I stayed close to my uncle and aunt as we watched the men who were to play the next day dance in a circle around a fire shouting to the beat of a gourd rattle. Uncle John pointed out that the seven women who danced and chanted to the echoing measure of a drum represented the seven clans. They didn't smile and didn't touch as they wove in and out of the dancers. It was so beautiful I didn't want to look away, but there was something a little scary about it, too.

I asked why everyone looked so unhappy and was told this was a serious ceremony and the game was important to them. For several days before the game, my uncle said, the players were not allowed to eat certain foods or to have contact with a woman or an infant as they thought it would weaken them. I wondered what gave them such an idea, but of course it was all new to me.

The game began at noon the next day and was played with two long sticks with netting made of animal skin on the ends. The ball, called an anetsa, was a walnut-sized rock covered with deer hide and the goal was for the team to drive the ball between the two goal posts of the opposing side. Or, it seemed to me, to survive without killing each other.

The players wore breechcloths and covered themselves with grease streaked with paint and charcoal, and some had made ornaments of deer's tails, eagle feathers and snake rattles. Aunt Nancy said it was to make them look threatening. It worked.

I covered my eyes when one of the players was dragged away after being picked up and thrown to the ground. No one seemed to pay attention to him after that and I saw him limp away to be replaced by another player.

I don't think anyone noticed when Callie, Kate, and I tired of the game and slipped away to build stick houses in a grove of shade trees nearby. The game was finally over when one side scored twelve runs, and by that time the sun was low in the sky. My uncle and aunt hurried us home after that and I didn't object. I could tell some of men had begun to drink as I could smell alcohol in the air.

The next morning we woke to curious stillness, I suppose because most were tired after the festivities of the previous days. Uncle John had left for the print shop and my aunt rose early to do the washing outside in a big cast iron pot. I was helping her hang the rinsed laundry along the fence posts when Callie raced into the yard looking like a demon was on her trail.

She was out of breath from running and I didn't have to look at her twice to know something was wrong. My first thought was of little Awinita who loved to tease by trying to run away.

"What is it?" When I got closer I could see she'd been crying. "Tell me! Is everyone all right?"

Holding onto the fence railing, she nodded, gasping. "Yes—well, no! It's Tassel! The poor dog's terrified of loud noises—can't stand thunder—and you know how deafening it was yesterday with all the drumming and shouting. He wasn't there when we got home last night but I thought he'd turn up in the morning . . . and, oh, Nell, I just know he's run off somewhere! I'm afraid I'll never find him."

I knew how much my friend loved her dog. Her grandfather, who had died the year before, had given her Tassel as a puppy when Callie was small and the pet was special in more ways than one.

"Where do you think he might have gone?"

She shook her head, braids flying. "He could be anywhere—could've wandered off into the woods, and the river's not far away you know."

I didn't remind her that most dogs could swim and that Tassel had no reason to try and cross the river as I was sure she was aware of that. Callie was scared, and she was worried, and I didn't blame her.

"Help me hang out the rest of this washing, I'll go with you," I told her, trying to sound positive. "We'll find him, Callie. Don't worry."

But then, I didn't know what was going to happen later.

Chapter Twenty

"He's probably just hiding somewhere," I said as we climbed the fence where cattle grazed, and crossed to the edge of the woods. I remembered how scared I was when Gulliver ran after another dog one day and had "traveled" all the way to the other side of town before my brother finally found him.

Callie, running ahead, began to call out, and I joined her, shouting until my throat felt like I'd swallowed a thistle. We jumped a ditch where bees hovered over a tangle of wild daisies, and waded through a patch of brambles. A soft wind ruffled the grass and brought the sweet smell of summer as we stepped into the welcome shade.

"Has he ever gone this far before?" I asked when we rested later on a fallen log. Brambles had scratched through my stockings and I used my day cap to mop my hot face. It must be getting close to noon; at least that's what my stomach thought.

Callie shook her head. "I don't know . . . I don't think so. She twined a stem of grass around her finger and swatted away a fly. "There's a stream somewhere around here—on the other side of that little hill over there I think. "Maybe he got thirsty and was looking for a drink."

That sounded like a good idea to me as my throat

was so dry it was hard to swallow. "Then let's go see if we can find him." I offered my hand and pulled her to her feet. "Are you sure you know the way?"

"I think so. Seems I remember passing under a big old hemlock when I came here once with Papa looking for a lost calf. It was right on the edge of a shallow gully."

"Did you find it?" I asked.

"Find what?"

"The lost calf."

She nodded. "She was all tangled up in some undergrowth."

"Then, come on. Maybe we'll find Tassel, too," I said.

We hurried around the next slope, and then the next, but no big hemlock came in sight. "Maybe this isn't the right direction," I suggested, trying to ignore the rumble in my stomach.

Callie hesitated at the top of a rise, fingering her necklace as she looked about. "It can't be far . . . maybe that way?" And, taking a deep breath, she continued around a bend of the hill, calling the dog's name. I followed as closely as I could, years of pine straw crunching underfoot.

I found her sitting on a stone scratching the ground with a stick. "I wish we'd brought something to eat," I said. "I'm hungry."

She squinted up through the trees. "So am I. It must be well after noon. I was in such a hurry to find Tassel this morning I didn't eat any breakfast . . ." Callie slid a hand into her apron pocket and smiled, bringing out a baked sweet potato wrapped in corn husks. "I almost forgot about this."

I think it was the best sweet potato I'd ever tasted as we shared it sitting in the soft grass beneath a sassafras tree. We even licked the oozing syrup from the parched husks, and I broke off a tender stem from a lower branch of the tree and chewed it to help quench my thirst. If I hadn't still been hungry I think I could've curled up and gone to sleep in the grass.

"I'll bet Tassel will be there waiting when we get back," I said in an attempt to bring a smile to her solemn face.

"Maybe. I hope so, and I'm afraid Mother's going to be awfully worried. I don't think I even told her where I was going when I when I ran off this morning."

But I had told Aunt Nancy, I reminded her. I also remembered she had warned us not to go far.

"I wish we'd told someone where we were going to look." She sighed. "I think we'd better head back, Nell."

"We can come back later if he hasn't shown up." I hoped she remembered which way we'd come because I hadn't.

It didn't take long for both of us to realize Callie hadn't either. "Do you remember seeing these?" I asked, pointing to a scattering of tiny yellow lilies tucked away in a the shade.

"We probably just missed them," she said. I didn't think so.

We followed a low rise that took us through a pine thicket, and at any other time I would have taken pleasure in its spicy fragrance but I was in a hurry to get out the other side because I couldn't remember *it* either.

It felt good to be again in the sunlight where we stopped to examine the raggedy purple passion flowers we called maypops growing in a tousle of dark green vines. Later in the summer, the green egg-sized fruit would turn yellow and be ready to eat. When strained and simmered with sugar, the tart pulp made jelly that made your tongue tingle.

"Look, Nell!" Callie shouted, after we had wandered a little farther. "I've found blackberries!"

The thorny thicket of blackberry bushes grew along a deep furrow in the hillside. There they were—sweet, plump, and juicy—just waiting for us to come along and pick them. And so we did.

"Watch out for snakes," Callie warned me. "They like blackberries, too."

After that, I was careful where I stepped, and we crammed our mouths with berries until our hands and faces were stained with the juice.

"I wish we had something to put them in," Callie said after we had eaten our fill. Luckily we noticed a yellow poplar tree growing nearby and discovered we could make kind of a basket from its leaves.

By this time it was impossible not to notice dark clouds screening the sun, and a rumble of thunder reminded us we'd better look for shelter.

But where to go? Papa had always told me it wasn't safe to stand under a tree during a lightening storm, but if you were caught out in the open, wouldn't that be dangerous, too?

We ran for a grove of trees on a slight slope just ahead as the sky boiled into the color of ashes and wind began to whip the leafy branches. A small rabbit darted through the tall grass and disappeared, and birds took shelter in the thick brush.

The trees turned out to be young maples, and we headed for the one that had two lower limbs Callie said were close enough together to use as support for a roof. At her direction, we looked for fallen branches on the ground that were long enough to reach from limb to limb, then crisscrossed more limbs to cover. Grabbing handfuls of brush and leaves, we piled that on top, but had trouble keeping it from blowing away.

"We need to find something heavy to hold this down," Callie said, looking about. The first rain drops were beginning to spatter around us and I remembered seeing a large piece of bark from a fallen log in a little dip in the hillside. It should be just the thing.

I found it covered with the pink and white rabbit peas that Uncle John called goat's rue and tugged at it until a piece came away—just as the first lightening streaked from the sky.

Callie struggled to hold down our clumsy attempts at a roof with both hands. "Hurry!" she shouted.

And I did, but I guess I forgot to look where I was going because my foot sank into a hole throwing me face down on the grass.

Well, at least I managed to hold onto the slab of bark, I thought, clumsily struggling to my feet. That was when I discovered it was painful to walk.

"What happened? Are you hurt?" Callie asked, noticing my limp.

"Stepped into a hole—must've twisted my ankle." We hurried to secure our hasty cover and crawled inside. There was just enough space for the two of us to sit if we didn't move around. Thunder rolled closer and rain began to ooze through our ceiling. We huddled together, reaching out with cupped hands to catch enough water to drink.

Together, Callie and I tugged off my boot as my

ankle had begun to throb, and it hurt even more when I touched it.

"I'm afraid it's going to swell," she said.

How was I going to get back if I couldn't put weight on my foot?

I peeled off my torn stocking, and with Callie's help, wrapped it around my ankle as tightly as I could, remembering how Dr. Means had bound Tom's wrist when he fell out of a tree.

"A poultice of mashed-up acorns might keep the swelling down," Callie suggested. "That's what my grandmother uses."

But her grandmother wasn't here and I doubted if either of us wanted to go out in the rain and smash up acorns.

We inched up with our backs against the tree and sat close together as wind reached for us and rain made puddles on our "floor."

"Nell, I'm sorry." Callie hugged herself, shivering.

"It's not your fault."

"Yes, it is. I shouldn't have wandered away like that. I thought I knew where I was going, and now you're hurt, we're both wet, and it's freezing out here."

"Well," I reasoned, "I didn't *have* to come along."

Her eyes were as dark and sad as the weather. "I know," she said, reaching once more for the necklace that seemed to bring her courage. "Let's take time about telling stories. Maybe we won't think about being so cold."

Callie went first. "Did you know that when the world was young, the rabbit had a long bushy tail?" she began.

"He bragged about it so much all the other animals

got tired of hearing it, so one winter day when the lake froze over, Fox went down there and cut a hole in the ice, tied some fish to his tail, and dropped it into the cold water.

"He didn't have to wait long before here came Rabbit wanting to know what he was doing.

"'Fishing,' Fox said. 'Don't you know this is the best way?' And he pulled out his tail to show him all the fish.

"Rabbit thought that was a fine idea, so as soon as Fox hurried away with his fish, Rabbit took his place, sinking his beautiful bushy tail into the icy lake. He fished and he fished, but without any luck, and the next morning when he tried to get up, he was frozen fast.

"Of course Fox had been waiting for that, and when he came along, Rabbit was chattering from cold and begged for help to get him unstuck.

"So Fox gave him a great big shove from behind, and Rabbit shot out of that hole and landed with a plop all the way on the other side of the lake.

"Of course," Callie added, "his tail was still frozen in the water—and that's why the rabbit now has only a little puff of a tail."

I rubbed my hands together for warmth. "Don't you know any stories about *warm* places?"

She managed a shivery laugh. "All right, it's your turn now."

When I was little, Papa had read me fairy stories, taking care to try and make each voice just right, and although I'd never admit it to him, Aunt Ida was even more believable.

Her favorite was *Jack and the Beanstalk*. I had come to the "fee-fi-fo-fum" scary giant part when the wind picked up, sending a limb crashing nearby.

Callie and I grabbed each other at the same time. "I guess we need to think of some different stories," she said.

But how can you think when you're wet and chilled, and how can you talk when you're trembling with cold? "Maybe if we *think* warm, we'll *be* warm," I suggested. "Let's pretend we're wrapped in a soft wooly blanket . . ."

"Stretched out with our feet to the fire," Callie continued. "Let's put on another log . . ."

Maybe pretending worked because I closed my eyes, and when I opened them, the rain had eased, but darkness had come in its place. And Callie was gone.

Chapter Twenty-One

I crawled outside to find a soaking landscape the color of soot; the only sound, the slow, measured dripping of moisture from the trees. There was no sign of Callie. I shouted her name, and when no answer came, shouted again. Louder. Only silence screamed back.

Maybe she's gone for help, I reasoned, but my friend was as lost as I was and I didn't believe she would chance wandering alone in the dark. And besides, she wouldn't leave me. *What if something has happened to her?*

I was alone.

Suddenly I didn't seem to have enough breath, and my heart thudded so I felt it was going to jump right out of my chest. Favoring my injured ankle, I made my way to the edge of the grove and called out again but my words disappeared into darkness.

What if nobody found me? Papa was going to be sad if I died out here, I thought. But he wouldn't be nearly as sad as I. And hugging the nearest maple, I let the tears spill over, calling out to Papa and Lucy and God.

But not a one of them showed up.

And poor Callie! She might be lying somewhere injured, calling out for help, and I didn't know where to find her.

"I'll just have to wait until morning," I said to the

maple tree, as there was nobody else to listen. "If help doesn't come before then, I'll make myself a walking stick and find my own way back!"

"Who are you talking to? And what on earth are you doing out here?"

The familiar sound of Callie's voice was as welcome as a choir of angels . . . and considering my present situation, even more.

"I guess I'm talking to this tree since there's nobody else around. I've never been as glad to hear anyone in my life, and I'd hug you if I could just *see* you!"

"Stay there—I'm coming!"

I think that was the wettest hug I've ever had, but I didn't care one bit. The fabric of my friend's dress clung to her chest and her braids trailed tiny streams of water down the front.

"Where have you been?" I demanded. "I've been worried to death."

Arm in arm we struggled back to our better-than-nothing shelter and crawled inside.

"I was so cold . . . and we were both shivering, so I thought maybe I could find some dry wood and build a fire." Callie sighed. "I found some good tinder inside a fallen log, but I didn't have a flint, and I knew from watching others I'd have to have two pieces of dry wood to get it going . . . " She scrunched up into a ball and rubbed her arms. "I couldn't even find one piece of dry wood. I'm sorry, Nell."

"I'm just relieved to have you back. We'll find our way home when it's light."

"If we aren't found before then. I know our people are looking for us. They must be as frightened as we are."

I said I didn't know about that and Callie laughed. "How's your ankle?' she asked.

"Fat. And it hurts."

"We could surely use some help from the little people about now," she said after minutes of silence.

"What little people?"

"The Yunwi Tsundi. They're kind of like fairies and we can't see them, except for maybe once in a while, but they're here and they have magic powers."

"What kind of powers?"

"To help people—humans, I mean."

"We're human." I squinted into the darkness. If any were out there, I hoped they were aware of us. "Have you ever seen them?"

"No, but my uncle has, and my grandmother too. She said he was bathing in a puddle and wasn't any taller than her knee."

"Did she say anything to him?"

"Oh, no! You don't want to frighten them. If you annoy them, they won't help you."

"I think we must've annoyed them," I said, and Callie laughed.

"Well, if we did," she said, "I'm sorry."

Neither of us had any idea what time it was and it didn't seem to be getting any lighter outside. How long would we have to wait?

Then I remembered the alphabet game Miss Mary Rose had invented to keep me entertained on bad weather days; sometimes my brother joined in. We called it, "On My Farm," and I suggested to Callie it might help pass the time.

When Tom and I played, we tried to think of the most ridiculous animals to stock our farms, but neither Callie nor I had the energy to be inventive.

"On my farm, I'm going to have an antelope," I began. Callie followed with a buffalo. We had worked our way through chicken, duck, and elephant when she suddenly sat forward and called for quiet.

"I thought I heard something," she whispered after a few hold-your-breath moments.

I realized I was clenching my fists. "Like what?"

"There's something out there . . . some kind of animal. Don't you hear it?"

Something was moving through the underbrush, and it was moving fast. A deer? Or maybe a wile boar. Whatever it was, it was getting closer.

I know I screamed when the big furry animal crashed into our shelter, and so did Callie, but she'll never admit it. Whatever it was meant to eat both of us. I was certain of it, but I couldn't . . . wouldn't . . . look. Covering my eyes, I did my best to roll into a ball.

A wet mouth nuzzled my cheek, and the strange animal poked its long nose in my ear . . . and barked!

"Tassel! Oh, Tassel, you wonderful dog!" Laughing and crying at the same time, Callie threw her arms around his neck. And so did I.

What followed was the most beautiful sound of all: voices calling our names.

Tumbling from our tangled canopy, we were greeted by the fresh green smell of pitch and the welcoming blaze of a pine torch.

Later we were surprised to learn that it was only a little

after midnight when Tassel led Callie's father and brother and several others on a meandering three-mile search before finding us. They immediately fired shots to let others know we had been found as the group had dispersed in different directions, with my uncle and his party covering the area near the river.

When Tassel showed up without us early that afternoon, my aunt expected us to soon follow, but when the two of us had not returned by suppertime, their alarm grew. Bearing torches, searchers covered as many areas as possible, as daylight faded into night.

Callie insisted on walking back on her own, but I didn't object one bit when her father scooped me up and carried me safely over the rough terrain. "You did the right thing to remain where you were," he told us. "It took courage to stay as calm as you did."

"But I . . ." I had started to tell him I hadn't stayed all that calm, but I glimpsed my friend's secret smile when she glanced at me in the torchlight and let my words disappear in the air.

That night Aunt Nancy bathed and soothed my bites and scratches and soaked my swollen ankle in an extract made from boiling the stems and leaves of the witch hazel shrub. Pulling a light blanket around me, I crawled into bed and knew nothing more until noon.

Chapter Twenty~Two

"I've brought you something to do," Callie announced when she showed up on our doorstep a few days later. For the past couple of days, my time had been spent playing with Helen, peeling vegetables, and letting the hems down on several small dresses that belonged to the Boudinot and Worcester children. Tasks like this, my aunt explained, were passed around to make light of the work that seemed to constantly accumulate.

I was so happy to see my friend, I didn't care what she brought as long as it had nothing to do with sewing.

"What's the matter with your arm?" I asked, noticing a rough red rash.

She groaned. "Poison ivy. We've been treating it with leaves from the touch-me-not plant. It looks bad, but it doesn't itch like it did."

"We're a pair, aren't we? I'm limping around, you have a rash, and we're both covered in bites and scratches."

But we agreed it could've been worse, and Callie's mother had sent along a project to help us think of something else.

In a pail, she carried coils of honeysuckle vines her mother had harvested and stored in the winter. Callie explained they had been soaked and the bark removed to expose the white skin beneath, and she was going to teach me how to weave a basket.

Aunt Nancy helped us get started by crossing four

of the vines for the bottom of the basket and lashing them together with a piece of fiber to make seven in all. These she called warps, and the vines were woven in and out in a circular pattern to make the bottom of the basket, then continued as we raised the sides. When the sides were high enough, the vines had become brittle so we left them to soak for a little while. To make a handle, Callie showed me how to bend two opposite warps to the other side and wrap them together with vines. When finished, it was a little larger than a baby's bonnet, and I could hardly wait to use it.

"We should still be able to find blackberries," Callie told me. "When your ankle's better, we can go picking."

"As long as we don't get lost!" I said.

She laughed. "Or wander into poison ivy."

June sunshine splashed around us as we sat in the shade of a dogwood. Nearby, sweet lavender bloomed by the doorstep and the hollyhocks my aunt had planted from seed were already almost a foot high. Green-rinsed June promised golden summer days, but happiness stayed just out of reach. There was a heaviness here. Barefoot children chased one another through the grass. Their games were the same, but their laughter wasn't. Would their echoes linger after they were gone?

Although they didn't discuss it in my presence, I knew my uncle and aunt were worried about the growing divide between those agreeing with Boudinot, and his brother, Stand Watie, who felt their only choice was to accept the change and yield to matters over which they had no control, and those who supported Chief John Ross in his struggles to unite his people in opposing removal. Major Ridge, a respected leader, and his son John also agreed that removal was unavoidable. Even I could see this had created a crevice between the people so sharp it might have been carved with a knife.

That night my uncle brought home a letter from Papa. It was addressed to all of us, and I was relieved to hear his injuries had healed, and except for a slight limp, he was able to get about almost the same as before. If all went according to plan, he and my brother would come for me sometime around the middle of August.

My aunt stooped to check the hoecake baking on the hearth. "Oh, good! That means you'll be here for the Green Corn Dance."

The Green Corn dance, or Stomp Dance, she told me, was a festival to celebrate the beginning of the green corn season and offer thanks for the blessing. And if anyone needed a blessing, I thought, it would be my friends at New Echota.

I have interviewed several ladies, Papa wrote, *and found two I believe suitable for the governess position. The choice will between a Miss Lucretia Spencer from Macon and Miss Hortense Hogg of the Augusta area, and I hope to make a decision soon . . .*

Uncle John, who had been reading the letter aloud, began to cough until his face turned flaming red and tears streamed from his eyes.

At first I was alarmed, but then my aunt, who seemed to be trying her best not to smile, touched his arm. "John," she said. "John, stop it. That's enough now."

"Oh, dear! Oh, dear! Oh, dear!" My uncle took out his handkerchief and wiped his eyes, and bending double, shook again with laughter.

"The poor woman can't . . . she can't help . . ." My aunt began, and then, she, too, dissolved into laughter. And so did I. Minutes later, poor little Helen, unused to such a racket, woke crying and had to be comforted.

"Well," Uncle John said after things had settled down, "with a last name like that you'd think the lady's parents could have at least spared her the *Hortense.*"

Later, when I said my prayers, I asked God to please let Papa choose the governess with the pretty name. Maybe I should've felt guilty for asking for such a silly thing with all the troubles in the world.

But I hoped that maybe once in a while it wouldn't matter.

By the end of the week the swelling was gone from my ankle and Aunt Nancy thought it would be all right to go berry-picking.

Wearing bonnets to keep out the sun and long sleeves to protect us from thorns and insect bites, Callie and I set out early one morning to find the juiciest berries. I was glad I had carried a pail instead of my tiny basket because within an hour, it was almost full. With the two of us picking, we soon had enough for both families, and Callie suggested we share with the Boudinots.

"All this worry and debate about the removal has been hard for Mrs. Boudinot," Callie explained. "Her husband is advising we accept the terms of removal, and Chief John Ross is completely against it."

I knew my uncle was worried that Mr. Boudinot might be replaced as editor of *The Phoenix* because of the editorials he wrote in favor of leaving so it wasn't surprising that his wife would be upset.

"Mrs. Worcester and her children still share their home," Callie continued. "She's been so patient waiting for her husband to be released from prison, but just think how worrisome it must be for both families."

I held a thorny branch aside as we stepped carefully through the tangle of blackberry bushes, our pails full. "What do your parents think?" I asked.

Callie waited until we were clear of the clawing vines to answer. "My father fought with the Cherokee Brigade under John Ross when Chief Ross was a lieutenant in the Battles of Talladega and Horseshoe Bend. Andrew Jackson was a general then, and together, with Jackson's volunteers, they defeated the Creeks. It was with their help, Jackson was able to declare victory." Stepping into the shade of a sycamore, she turned to me. "My parents think President Jackson has a short memory," she said.

We found both Mrs. Worcester and Mrs. Boudinot at the Boudinot home working quietly at a quilting frame while one of the older cousins kept the younger children entertained with rag dolls. The women were happy to get the berries and declared there would be more than enough for a pie.

"How do you go about making a pie?" Callie wanted to know. I remembered Patsy's good blackberry cobblers and pies but had no idea how to make one.

"Why don't the two of you come over tomorrow afternoon and we'll have a pie-making session?" Miss Harriett offered.

We left our pails of berries in their spring house

until we returned the next day for our pastry-making lesson. After mixing butter, flour, salt, and water to make the pie shells, we found the hardest part was rolling it out so it didn't stick to the rolling pin or fall apart before we could fit it in the pan, but our teachers only laughed and said nobody would be the wiser if the dough was patched together. After the pastry was finally laid in cast iron skillets, we added the washed berries with sugar, flour, nutmeg, and more butter before covering with a top crust. Finally, the four of us had as many pies ready to go into the big bake oven beside the fireplace. Our kitchen had one like that at home, but Aunt Nancy baked in the fireplace itself, as did Callie's mother.

"Come back in about an hour or so," Mrs. Boudi-not told us after we had helped clean up all the mess. "The pies should be ready by then and cool enough to take home."

"You look like a ghost," Callie told me as we walked home together. "You have flour all over your face."

I laughed. "So do you!" And we flapped our flour-flecked aprons to make a summer "snow" storm.

The pies tasted as good as they smelled, and my aunt and uncle declared they had never eaten anything better. Even little Helen smacked her lips over a few spoons full of the gooey juice.

My tiny cousin was developing into a person in her own right. She could now stand, holding to a chair, and loved to "walk" holding onto our hands. Her fawn-colored hair was a soft tuft that stood straight up on her head, and she clapped her little hands and laughed at the mention of patty-cake. How was I ever going to leave her?

Chapter Twenty-Three

June was flowing through our fingers and corn was higher than my head in the fields outside of town. Callie hadn't talked again about leaving. It was almost as if she was afraid mentioning it would make it happen, but I had heard that Kate's friend Susannah and her family had left a few days earlier.

The path was streaked with sunlight and a light breeze ruffled the grass as Callie and I took our picnic of cold chicken and bread made of corn meal and mashed beans to our not-so-secret spot at the bent tree. Peaches were just beginning to ripen, and along the way, Mrs. Boudinot invited us to help ourselves to some of the fruit in their orchard. We picked a few for dessert, and they smelled so sweet I couldn't resist eating one of them first.

Pink Lady's Slippers bloomed in the surrounding woods and I planned to pick a few for the table before we started home. In a dense, low-lying area, we'd discovered a strange looking white plant Callie said was called Indian Pipes because of the shape. They grew in clusters and had no color, and would've been pretty, I guess, if they didn't make me feel kind of shivery. Callie said some people called them ghost plants and I could see why.

"It won't do any good to pick them," she said, "because if you do, they'll just turn black."

I didn't even want to touch them, but I'm glad we came upon them as I'd never seen anything like that before and probably never would again.

"Race you!" Callie shouted when we were in sight of the familiar oak that had been bent to mark a trail, and I picked up my skirts and ran to claim a seat on the limb beside her. Swinging our feet, we hung our basket of lunch on a nearby limb and shared its contents. Neither of us spoke for a time; maybe we were both wondering if this might be the last time we would come here. I wiped peach juice from my fingers with the napkin my aunt had tucked into our basket and offered it to Callie, but she seemed a million miles away.

"Listen," she said, her voice like a whisper. And so I did. Somewhere nearby two birds were calling to each other; a squirrel scampered through the leaves under-foot and disappeared into the foliage of a sweetgum tree. A cow mooed in a distant pasture.

"I don't hear anything," I said.

She turned to me and smiled. "Yes, you do. "It's the song of life. It's all around us—the music of the soul . . . just listen."

I started to tell her I couldn't hear any music, and that bothered me. Why could Callie hear these things when I couldn't? And then a robin sailed in and landed on a limb above us and sang out to let us know it was there; a frog led a chorus from the stream that twisted through the woods; bees hummed, weaving through the daisies, and a chipmunk sang soprano with its tiny high-pitched chip-chip. I laughed. "It's an orchestra! They're playing a symphony."

"And we're the audience. Just look around you,

Nell. We could be the only people in the world."

And for a few seconds we seemed to be wrapped in green, like the forest had put its arms around us. I felt its peace become part of me . . . and then it was gone. I wish it could've lasted forever.

Callie tossed a peach pit into the woods. "June is almost over. Before long it will be time for the Green Corn Dance."

She spoke like she dreaded it to happen. "I thought you were looking forward to it," I said.

"I was . . . I am." Suddenly she slid from her perch and jumped to the ground. "Come on! Let's see if we can find that bee tree Joseph was telling me about."

Did that mean her family planned to leave after the Green Corn Dance?

We found the tree and Callie pointed out the nest high up on the end of a limb. "My father says it's best to wait until most of the bees are gone to smoke out the rest and harvest the honey so we won't kill all the bees," she told me.

"When will that be?"

"Probably not until the end of summer." After both of us were gone, I thought, but neither of us said it aloud.

July brought a surge of energy and expectation to the village of New Echota—or most of it, anyway, as everyone got ready to celebrate the Green Corn Dance, sometimes called the Stomp Dance. From what I'd been told, I expected to see a lot of stomping taking place. The first week of the month was almost over before I realized no one had mentioned Independence Day.

Back home in Athens there were usually fireworks and speeches, and last year we had been invited to a barbecue, but the day went unnoticed here. We fought to win our independence from England; now the Cherokees and other tribes want independence from us. Just now their chances didn't look good. Papa had said he planned to run for office in the fall, but even if he were elected, it might be too late to help their cause.

"People should be arriving for the Green Corn Festival next week," my aunt said one day at supper.

I was trying to get Helen to take another bite of oatmeal but she didn't want any part of it. "What day are they having it?" I asked.

Uncle John laughed. "It's not just one day. The whole thing lasts a good part of a week—or as long as people want to stay."

Aunt Nancy explained that it was a celebration of thanksgiving to The Breath Maker for the first fruits of the harvest.

I frowned. "You mean God?"

She nodded. "Some call him Hsaketumese. People will come and set up their campsites the first day and the men will feast on whatever remains of last year's crop. After the Stomp Dance that night, they'll not eat anything for almost two days."

"Just the men?" I asked, glad it wouldn't be required of me.

"The ones who are taking part," my aunt said, "and it couldn't have come at a better time. The Festival, which is called Puskita, is meant to renew a sense of the sacredness of life and forgiveness. You might hear some refer to it as Busk."

The number in our village seemed to multiply overnight as people came from miles around to set up camp for the Green Corn Festival. Their cooking fires flickered and blazed as darkness came and everyone gathered for the Stomp Dance to begin.

After smoking the ceremonial pipe, the tribal elders and clan heads were invited to take part in the first dance. The song leader danced in front keeping the rhythm of the dance with shakers made of turtle shells. With their left hands toward the middle, they circled a center fire with stomping shuffling steps while another person kept time with a drum.

After the first dance, others were allowed to join in until it seemed almost all the men had taken part.

Aunt Nancy pointed out that no alcohol was allowed during this time as it was a sacred occasion, and in between the dances some of the religious leaders gave sermons to encourage good behavior, not only at festival time, but all year. I noticed the Reverend Bushyhead among others there.

The dancing lasted most of the night but we only stayed for a part of it. Aunt Nancy hadn't been feeling well lately and I tried to help her as much as I could. Helen had outgrown her cradle and now slept in a crib her father had made for her. She didn't seem happy if she wasn't allowed to crawl, and tried her best to walk holding onto to our hands or the furniture and had to be constantly watched. I made her a little pen by enclosing a space with benches and chairs, but she made it clear she wanted me to be inside it with her.

We woke the next morning to find four brush arbors set up in each direction where the activities were to take place and a fire was laid in the middle. This was where some of the new crop of corn, beans, and squash would be offered. Uncle John said it was to give thanks and atone for their sins. When it grew dark, it was the women's turn to dance wearing rattles made by putting pebbles in shells and tying them around their legs.

I asked my aunt why she wasn't taking part, and that's when I found out why she hadn't been feeling well.

"Women who are expecting aren't allowed to participate," she told me, smiling. "Helen is going to have a little brother or sister sometime after Christmas."

"But I won't be here then!"

She laughed. "Well then, I guess we'll just have to arrange for you to come for another visit."

I made a face. "But by then Papa will have hired another governess—probably the one with the awful name—and he'll never let me come."

Aunt Nancy stooped to give me a hug. "Then we'll just have to visit you."

"Really? Do you think you might come to Athens?"

"Your uncle and I have talked about it, and there's a possibility that sometime next summer, when the baby is old enough to travel, we might make the trip."

"Oh, that would be wonderful! I've so much to show you, and you can have the room right next to mine."

It wasn't that I didn't want to go home. I missed Papa and Lucy—sometimes I missed them so much it hurt, and Patsy, too—even Thomas, and of course my sweet Gulliver, but I hated to leave my new "other family" behind, especially Helen who had become like a little sister to me. Uncle John had written Papa about

Callie and me getting lost. He felt it was his duty, he said, and Papa wrote me a long letter about how I should always stay close to the village, and I was to give my word not to wander off again. I could tell it worried him a lot, and that made me feel sad . . . and that's exactly why I wished my uncle would've kept it to himself. Sometimes I wonder if grownups *ever* think things through.

The third night the men were to dance the Feather Dance, to heal the community, my aunt said. Cherokees don't wear feathers or headdresses made of them. Sometimes the men might wear one or two, usually somewhere near the top of the head, so I was curious to see what kind of dance this would be.

We were on our way to join to crowd to watch the dance when Callie ran up to me and caught me by the hand, and I could tell with one look something awful must have happened.

"I've lost my necklace! Can you help me look?"

I started to ask where she lost it, but realized what a silly question that would be. If she knew where she lost it, she would've found it by now. "When did you see it last?" I asked.

"I know I had it on this morning, but just noticed it was gone." She clasped her hands to her chest where the necklace usually rested. "It could be anywhere!"

"Then let's go over where you've been today," I said, leading her aside. It was early afternoon and the dance was due to begin soon, but the necklace was a gift from her grandmother and I knew how much it meant to my friend.

"First I went to the spring," she said, "but I've looked there—looked all around, and it's not there.

Then Awinita wanted to play ball with Tassel so I spent a while outside with her . . ."

"*Where* outside?"

"Just around our house, but I've looked there, too—front and back. Oh, Nell, I don't know what I'll do if I've lost it! It was a special gift, and I—"

"I know, and we're going to find it," I said, hoping I wouldn't be wrong. "Let's go over the places where you and Awinita were playing. Maybe you just missed seeing it in the grass." I had never seen Callie cry, but it was clear she was close to tears.

But after almost an hour spent combing the grassy area around her house, we still hadn't found the missing necklace.

"It's not here, Nell. We might as well give up." Callie stood, shoulders sagging, and attempted to shake out the grass stains on her skirt.

"Then it must be somewhere else. You did look in the house, didn't you?"

"Of course. I looked there first, and mother looked, too. Even Joseph. If it had been there, we would've found it."

"Then you lost it somewhere else. Where did you go after you played with Awinita?"

"Straight to the place where everybody was gathering to watch the dance. That's when I saw you . . . and I've looked around there, too."

I frowned. "And you didn't go anywhere else?"

"No. I told you, I—

"No, wait! Mother forgot a basket while she was in the cornfield yesterday picking beans, and I went back there this morning to get it, but I was only there for a minute."

"It only takes a minute to lose a necklace," I told her, but she had already started running to the field behind their house where corn, beans and squash had been planted.

I caught up with her at the gate.

"The basket was there," Callie said, pointing to the far end of the first row. "She'd already filled another but didn't need the second one and just forgot it in her hurry."

The two of us walked slowly down the row of cornstalks. Beans had been planted to climb the stalk at the bottom of about every other one. Near the end of the row, I found the necklace hanging midway up a stalk of corn and snatched it up. "That's strange," I said, dangling it so she could see. "I guess this must've grown here."

Chapter Twenty-Four

"Oh, Nell!" Callie threw her arms around me. "I'd feel awful if I lost that necklace. I was afraid I'd never see it again. Thank you!"

"You would've found it if I hadn't seen it first. I'm just glad you have it back."

"It must've come untied." Callie used her apron to blot away tears. "I guess we missed the Feather Dance."

And we had, of course, but neither of us seemed to mind. Later, when it was time for supper, word was passed that food had been prepared and the men could now end their fasting. We watched as they walked in single file to meet and wash in the river. Uncle John said it was to wash away illness and bad thoughts. Afterward, they returned for a Stomp Dance before feasting.

The Green Corn Ceremony was a time when debts and grudges were forgiven, as were other transgressions, with the exception of murder. I learned that corn was an important crop to the Cherokees as it was considered to be a symbol of life and a special gift from the Creator.

Later, over bowls of soup made of corn, beans, and hominy, Aunt Nancy told me about the legend of Selu, the Corn Mother, who was said to be the first woman.

"You mean like Eve from the Bible?" I said.

She nodded. "Except that Selu was believed to have been created from an ear of corn, and as goddess of the corn, she symbolizes the bounty of the earth."

And, in keeping with tradition, the village continued to celebrate that bounty by feasting and dancing far into the night. I thought most would be too tired to do anything but rest the next day, but my uncle said there would be more dancing and games before everyone packed up to go home.

A game of stickball began soon after noon the following day, followed by a game they called marbles, or Digadayosdi, played with billiard balls on a field of about a hundred feet. Callie's brother Joseph was on one of the teams and she and I watched it together to cheer for them. Five holes about two inches wide and ten yards apart had been made in an L shape on the playing field, and players took time about tossing the balls at the holes. Once a player managed to get the ball in the fifth hole, he had to turn around and play in the opposite direction until he had scored ten holes in all. Callie said the balls used to be made of carved stone, and some still played with those, but I didn't see any like that. Each team was made up of three people and there were five teams so it took a long time for everyone to play, and it was almost dark before the game ended. I thought for a while Joseph's team might win, but another team finished before they did.

The festivities ended with a Friendship Dance in which both men and women took part. Dancers were led by a singer with a gourd rattle who was followed by a woman with tortoise shell rattles on her legs. Another man kept time with a skin drum as the dancers wound in a spiral moving faster and faster, ending with a lot of laughter. Callie pointed out that the dancers were young people who were getting to know one another, and they joked and clapped the whole time they were taking part. I thought it was a good way to end the Festival because everyone seemed happy. At least for a while. I was so tired I don't even remember crawling into bed that night.

For the next few weeks everyone stayed busy harvesting summer vegetables. Green beans were threaded on a string, then hung from rafters in kitchens or barns to dry for the months ahead. They were called "leather britches" because they looked like leather when dried, and when ready to eat had to be soaked a long time before cooking. Peas were dried, too, as were peaches and apples, and there were several ways to keep corn through the winter; one was to bind a few ears by the shucks and hang them suspended in a warm dry place. Root vegetables such as potatoes, winter squash, pumpkins, carrots, beets, and turnips could be kept for months in a root cellar or a pit dug for that purpose.

I remembered that Patsy had always had extra help in the kitchen during this time so we would have vegetables and fruits after the season was over, but we didn't take part in the harvesting. This summer would be different.

"Don't forget to wear your bonnet to keep out the sun," Aunt Nancy reminded me as I took my basket and started for the garden. Summer squash wouldn't keep and had to be picked and used right away, and the small cucumbers would be stored in barrels of brine to make tart, crunchy pickles. Fresh corn was either boiled and served on the cob with butter or fried with bacon, but most of the crop was saved for later. Even the stalks and shucks were used for fodder, and cobs made kindling for the fireplace.

I didn't see Callie much during this time as she and her family were doing the same things we were. At the edge of her garden, my aunt had planted colorful flowers she called "old maids." They were higher than my waist and looked a lot like daisies, but were all different colors. I picked enough for a pitcher for the table and had more left for another. Aunt Nancy agreed that we should share with a neighbor, so that afternoon I took some to Callie and her family.

Callie greeted me at the door and invited me inside, and the first thing I noticed was strings of "leather britches" hanging from their rafters. Surely this was a good sign, meaning the family meant to stay through another winter. I was glad to see Callie wearing her necklace again after the ties had been replaced. She and her mother were shelling field peas into a large pan, now almost full. I offered to help while Callie found a container for the flowers, and watched how quickly her mother pried open each brown pod to release the peas.

It took a few tries before I caught onto the rhythm, but I liked feeling the small peas roll through my fingers and rattle into the pan. It was almost like opening a gift, and in a way, I suppose it was.

"Mother, tell us the story of your elisi and the little people," Callie said after we had filled two pans.

Setting the pan aside, her mother smiled. "It wasn't *my* elisi, but my grandmother's," she said, explaining that the word *elisi* means grandmother in Cherokee. "If she were my father's grandmother, she would be called *Enisi*," she added, "and this happened many, many years ago.

"Her name was Woya," she continued, "and she was a small girl—probably a few years younger than you

—and she had waded across a shallow stream to pick berries on the other side.

"She was so busy filling her basket, she didn't notice a storm was coming, and before she knew it, it began to rain, and it was a bad storm with a lot of wind and lightening. Woya was wet . . . and she was cold . . . and she was frightened. Then she noticed a large rock jutting from the side of the hill to make a shelf, so she gathered her basket and hurried to the overhang to take shelter from the rain."

"Poor Woya! What happened then," Callie urged, becoming impatient.

Her mother laughed. "You know very well what happened then. You've heard this story so many times, my daughter, you could tell it yourself."

"But I like the way you tell it." Callie turned to me. "This is the best part."

"Well," her mother said, "by the time the storm blew over, the stream had swollen until it was too wide and too deep for her to cross, so Woya stood on the side and called out for help. The current was so swift and she was so small, she knew she would be swept away if she tried.

"At first nothing happened, so she shut her eyes tight and called out again, and in a few minutes she heard a splash at her feet. Looking down, she saw a small limb about two feet long and about as thick as a hoe handle, and it was tied in the center to a vine. The wood had gotten snagged on a rock at her feet, and when she looked further, Woya saw that it was attached to a tree on the other side.

"And that's when she saw the little people!" Callie said.

"Whose story is this?" Her mother shook her head. "They came out from the underbrush, and there appeared to be several of them, as many as seven or eight, and they motioned for her to grab the stick and they would pull her across the stream.

"Woya was afraid because she'd heard the little people were fond of playing tricks, especially if they thought someone had done them wrong, but she knew she hadn't done this, so she grabbed the limb and stepped into the swirling water. She felt mud and rocks beneath her feet and began to wade through the waist-deep water one step at a time while the little people tugged on the vine from the other side. By the time she reached the middle, the water was almost up to her neck, but Woya held on tightly and began to kick as she'd seen her brothers do, and the more she kicked, the faster she moved until she could feel her feet touch the soggy bottom.

"Shivering with cold, Woya slowly made her way up the bank and on to dry land, but when she looked around to thank the little people who had helped her, they had all disappeared."

Although it was the end of July and we were sitting by a fire, I felt shivery myself. "I wonder what they looked like," I said.

"I doubt if they were even as tall as Awinita," Callie's mother said. "But Woya said they all had long hair, and she didn't remember them wearing any clothes."

I said I thought they must have been cold in the winter, and Callie added that there was something about that story she'd always wanted to ask.

Her mother emptied the shelled peas into a basket. "And what would that be?"

Callie laughed. "What happened to all the berries?"

I saw my friend only a few times after that: once or twice for a short visit at the spring, and for a little while after church one Sunday. July melted into August and Elias Boudinot resigned as editor of *The Phoenix*, writing to Chief John Ross that he couldn't consent to remain in that post without having the right to discuss both sides of the removal question.

Ross accepted his resignation and appointed his brother-in-law Elijah Hicks as editor.

It was a sad time. Sad for my aunt, troubled over her brother; sad for my uncle because he cared about the newspaper and the man who had given birth to it. Sad for Ann Worcester whose missionary husband still remained in prison in Milledgeville with Dr. Butler, and for Harriet Boudinot, furious that not only had her husband had been dismissed, but his patriotism attacked.

The state of Georgia had begun surveying Cherokee land with the intention of dividing it into parcels to raffle, and many families, although they didn't understand why this was taking place, decided to leave and take their chances somewhere else. I couldn't blame them.

We received a letter from Papa to let us know he had employed a governess—not, thank goodness—the one with the awful name. He and Thomas planned to arrive sometime in the middle of August to take me back to Athens in time for my brother to begin his second year at Franklin College, and I felt I was being pulled in two directions. Part of me was reluctant to leave the people I cared about here at New Echota, and the other part was eager to put the sadness behind me and step back into my old life.

But I would never be the Nell Kiziah Webb who had resented being made to come here. I knew now that whatever happened to New Echota, the people and the village would always live in a special place in my heart.

My stockings were wearing thin and I was on my way to the store for more when I saw it hanging by our gate.

Has Callie lost her necklace again? But what a strange place to find it! Why was in hanging on a fence post?

Carefully, I gathered it up in my hands. The ties had been replaced, and there didn't seem to be anything wrong with the new ones. Forgetting my errand, I ran to my friend's house with a feeling that I'd swallowed something big and it was stuck right in my middle, and the closer I came, the knowing grew stronger. The silence struck me like a hammer. No Tassel ran out to greet me; no smoke rose from the chimney. Chickens are rarely quiet, but I heard no clucking or crowing from their pen behind the house.

The family had left. I knew it—of course I knew it, but I had to be sure. The closed front door had a final look about it, but I knocked anyway and called out— not just to Callie, but to anyone who might still be there. When no one answered, I opened the door and stepped inside. A bare table stood in the middle of the floor with a chair at either end; a broom leaned against the fireplace, but everything else was gone: the rocking chair, the churn and spinning wheel—even the big iron cooking pot. They were on their way to somewhere else.

And so was Callie.

I keep in my heart the memory of my last time with

my friend in this place: the warmth of the fire, the thudding of peas, tiny Awinita napping beside us, her doll tucked under her chin; the story-telling, and the laughter. And most of all, the belonging.

I didn't cry until I reached home. Aunt Nancy must have sensed something wasn't right because she met me at the door.

"She's gone! Callie's gone, and the house is empty!" I cried, throwing myself in her arms. "I'll never see her again."

She didn't seem surprised. "They're on their way to Arkansas to make a new life, Nell. They probably left well before dawn. We must wish them Godspeed and a fresh beginning."

I did. Of course I did, but that didn't make it hurt less. "But she left her necklace, Aunt Nancy. It was a gift from her grandmother and I know how much it means to her. How can I ever get it back to her?"

She shook her head and smiled. "The necklace is for you. Callie's grandmother gave it to her because she held a special place in her heart. Now, Callie is passing it along to you, and one day, when you find someone who is worthy of the gift, you'll do the same."

My aunt lifted my braids and carefully tied the necklace around my neck and I fingered the colorful beads as my friend had done. It felt right there.

"But we never said goodbye," I said. "I didn't even have the chance to tell her goodbye."

Aunt Nancy smiled. "In the Cherokee language, there's no word for goodbye."

About the Author

No Word for Goodbye is Mignon F. Ballard's 22nd published book and the second for middle grade readers. Seven mysteries in the Augusta Goodnight series were followed by five set during WWII featuring first grade teacher, Miss Dimple Kilpatrick. Her last, *Miss Dimple and the Slightly Bewildered Angel,* features both series title characters. Her nine stand-alone books include *The Christmas Cottage, The War in Sallie's Station, Minerva Cries Murder, Final Curtain, The Widow's Woods, How Still We See Thee Lie, Cry at Dusk, Raven Rock, and* her only other book for young readers, *Aunt Matilda's Ghost.*

She lives in her hometown of Calhoun Georgia, where she is a volunteer at New Echota, the restored capital of the Cherokee Nation, located a few miles from her home.